Shattered Reality

A Blurring Reality Prequel

R. D. Chapman

Copyright © 2024 by Reneé D. Chapman
www.ShadesOfFall.com

Editor: Ray Rhamey
Cover Design: SelfPubBookCovers.com/thrillerauthor

Shades of Fall Publishing
ISBN: 979-8-9906998-1-6

A warm thank you to my family for their support and advice, especially beta readers Jack and Tara. A very grateful thank you to my editor, Ray Rhamey.

Chapter 1

Were any other interstellar civilizations held together by overstuffed flying sausages? Jem grumbled, wedging another package into the UPMS mail pod. This is what she got for not waiting until Dani got off work to meet up with her. Turning, she found two more packages being waved at her.

"For Pete's sake, Dani, this frigging sausage is about to puke," Jem said, glaring down at her friend. "Why don't you just fire up another one?"

Dani snorted. "The Euphrates System usually does need two but you're *suuuch* a good packer—"

"Stuffer."

"—I was pretty sure we could save the expense of the second one tonight. And that's the last of it," she said, handing them up.

Shooting her friend a you-owe-me glare, Jem was studying the packed interior when a pulse of…*something* went through her, as if a giant hand was twisting her insides.

* * * * *

"Marion! Dr. L!" Angie called out from her station in the laboratory. "I'm getting sensor fluctuations from the secondary test site. Maybe we're finally going to get some action."

* * * * *

A sudden weakness had her leaning against the mail pod for support…then the feeling dissipated just as quickly and her strength returned. *Okay, what was that?* Couldn't have been from skipping lunch. Shaking it off, Jem scrunched a satchel bearing a bank logo and a box from a candy company against the rear wall. That opened a large enough spot to wedge the two new ones in. She locked the cover into place and climbed down the short ladder.

Jem frowned as she headed toward the next pod. The pallet behind it wasn't stacked high enough to warrant a two-seater. UPMS had either run out of the smaller pods or—

"Antarius System. Got a courier scheduled for it," Dani called out.

Yep. That. "Want me to set it up?" Jem asked.

"You remember how?" When Jem gave her a mock-angry stare, Dani laughed and told her to go ahead. "I'll start loading the front."

Jem used a grabber to lift and trundle a bench seat from the hanger's storage area and carefully placed it in the pod's rear cargo section. Climbing in, she snuggled the seat into position against the back wall and locked it into place. Hearing voices, she popped her head up to see Dani and a man chatting in front of the mail pod's nose. Figuring it to be the courier, she went back to getting things prepped for him.

* * * * *

"Redlining!" Jonnie yelled from his position. Angie gave a choked-off scream as her station exploded with a bright flash of heat, smoke, and a frightening display of sparks.

* * * * *

Jem was connecting the oxygen line when the hair on her arms and neck suddenly stiffened. A wave, a shiver—that *something* again—but this time it was *huge*. Her body hunched as it arced through her from fingertips to toes. *What the hell?*

Hell answered.

Did she scream? She couldn't tell. A whirling maelstrom of blackness enveloped her in waves of agony that overwhelmed every thought. Ripping through her. Twisting her inside out. It ended as abruptly as it began.

Everything hurt. Her head spun like a carnival ride. She was half buried under debris and…she blinked, trying to focus. That, that was part of the pod's hatch across her chest. Had a shuttle crashed into the hanger? She heard voices. Shouts. Jem turned her head, almost losing the battle with her stomach. There…sticking up out of a debris pile next to her. Dani's hand. She recognized the ring, despite blurred and double vision. Was Dani alive? Arms and legs shoved debris aside as she inched sideways slowly, swallowing nausea-threatened bile. She reached out and grasped the bloody hand. Gave it a tug.

"Dani? Are you…"

She was holding a hand. Just a hand. It ended just past the wrist: white bone showing among the tattered strips of skin and—

Jem slung it away. Rolling on her side, she let her stomach have its way.

"*Shit, shit, shit.*"

She heard a frantic male voice over her heaving.

"*Dr. Bluethon. Over here!*"

Doctor? Jem tried to raise her head, but pain exploded from her skull and arrowed down her spine. This time, she felt nothing when the blackness pulled her down.

***

…fire. She was on fire. Her back arched and she screamed out her agony…

…she stumbled, fell. Dug her hands into dirt trying to find something solid to hang on to in the dipping, twirling world. Her stomach heaved…

…clawed hands reaching for her…glassy-eyed, two-headed monsters…

…a woman holding a bottle to her parched lips…

… a smiling Dani waving a handless arm…

…pain…more pain…

Chapter 2

Jem struggled against the returning consciousness, reluctant to leave the painless refuge of nothingness. She lay on her side. Her head—if a block of wood could be called that—throbbed, but no sign of the near constant nausea and vertigo. *Yet*. She moved a leg. Felt a brief twinge, but no pain or sudden spasms. *Yet*. She carefully opened her eyes. Blinking, trying unsuccessfully to focus, she slammed them shut when the room started a slow spiral.

No, dammit! Stop it, she told herself.

Beginning a slow roll, her back muscles spasmed. Teeth gritted, she waited out the pain, then finished the roll onto her back. Tried opening her eyes again. Nope. Taking several shallow breaths, she fought the nausea and vertigo down.

When the hell is this going to stop?

For that matter, she thought grimly, how long has it been?

She searched through memories, some vague, like a woman holding a cup to her lips: water or something thicker, like a broth. Other memories weren't vague enough. Hallucinations. Nightmares? Jem shuddered, which triggered a volley of knife pricks down her arms and legs.

Cut this crap out, she commanded herself again. Which was about as successful a demand as her first one. The click of a door opening, followed by soft footsteps, drew her immediate attention. "Who's there?"

The footsteps came closer.

"Hello?" a male voice said, hesitantly. "You're awake?"

"Yes."

"Can you open your eyes without puking?"

No promises. She lifted her eyelids slowly until she could make out the blurry figure of a man beside the bed. She fought down a brief surge of stomach flipflops.

"How do you feel?" Another cautious question.

"Not sure," she answered honestly. "Weak…headachy…can't focus."

"Pain? Nausea?"

She swallowed. "Only when I move; both bearable, so far. Where am I? How long since…whatever?" From what she could see, it didn't look like a hospital room.

"You're in a private residence. Thirsty? Hungry?"

"Yes," she replied, ignoring a queasy rumble from her middle. "Who are you?"

"Name's Ruben Davis. You've not been able to eat regularly—or keep it—and we couldn't do an IV. I'll bring some water and something to eat. Just…stay put."

Jem blinked as the man hurried out. Stay put? Was that supposed to be bedside humor? Why was she in a private residence? As for how long, the sight of her wrist bones jutting out of thin arms told her it'd definitely been a while. A quick peek under the thin blanket revealed a set of new-looking over-sized tunic and pants. Loose wear, the better to change her, she thought with a flush of embarrassment. Oh well, it beat hospital wear. And her regular clothes were in her travel bag, which she'd left in a three-day locker at the bus station. It was undoubtedly racking up fees in the unclaimed baggage storage room.

After Davis returned, it took about ten painful minutes to recover from being propped up with several large pillows. Finally, she signaled him. He'd been prudently waiting on the side, waiting to see if the nausea won out.

He sat a tray across her legs. It held a plastic bottle of water and a bowl of soup.

"Liquids are all we've been able to get down you. Marion said to only give you water and broth until you can handle—and keep—solids."

Jem's stomach gave a good kind of pang at the odor rising from the bowl and her hunger roared awake. With easily ignored twinges from her arms, it didn't take long to empty the bowl. She licked her lips and gave Davis a hopeful smile. "Another one, please?"

He eyed her cautiously. "Stomach?"

"Behaving," she assured him. Several minutes later, she was rapidly demolishing another steaming bowl of goodness. "By the way, what's that thing around my ankle?" A wide metal band, similar to a few fancy bracelets she'd seen but thicker, wrapped around her left ankle. There were several slightly protruding oval sections around it.

"I've let the doctors know you're awake and lucid," Davis responded. "They'll be here shortly and will explain things."

Jem swallowed her current mouthful. "And they are?"

"Doctors Lammstein and Bluethon. Our project leaders."

She stilled. That didn't sound medical. "What project?"

Davis sighed. "The one that brought you here and blew up our lab."

Jem's startled "*What?*" bounced off his back as he left the room.

What did a blown-up lab have to do with what she remembered happening? A large chunk of it hitting the hanger, maybe? She frowned. No, what little she remembered was more like an explosion, not a crushing. Explanations would be good, she fumed, shoving an unwanted image of a hand away. She was still mulling it over when the door opened and admitted two people. Neither fit her idea of a doctor.

The man was medium height, dressed in jeans, a blue t-shirt under a jacket, and carried a high-backed kitchen chair. The woman was also medium height but wore a brown and green flannel shirt over brown cargo pants. Jem watched them cautiously as the woman settled into the chair Davis had used and the man set his chair next to her. The two shared a look and the man motioned toward Jem. Evidently that was a "you go first" signal.

The woman introduced them with a bright smile. "Hello. I'm Dr. Marion Bluethon and this is my associate, Dr. Enrique Lammstein. We are very glad to see you awake and aware. How is your pain level?"

"It only hurts when I move, and then mostly in my back."

"Excellent." Dr. Bluethon cleared her throat. "You had no ID on you when you…arrived. Could you tell us your name?"

Jem stared, nonplussed.

"We submitted a fingerprint scan," the man offered, "as if you were a possible hire-on, but it came back negative. No one has submitted a missing person report for you with Law Enforcement, either personally or in connection to the hanger explosion. We've, uh, checked for someone fitting your description."

"Bi-colored eyes did narrow down the search parameters, but we still didn't find you," the woman said, sounding a bit sheepish.

"Jem Seaborne Wilmont," she said slowly, looking between the two of them. "I have no close family and have been drifting, working odd jobs for several years. Nothing that required fingerprinting, and I've never been in trouble with the authorities." Suspicious, she asked, "You didn't request DNA identification for an unknown, unconscious patient?"

"No."

That would have required a formal Law Enforcement request. There were only a few reasons why they wouldn't have and none of them good. Her stomach knotted and her hands fisted. "Where the hell am I, how long have I been here, and what, exactly, is going on?"

They shared another, longer look. "You've been here just over four weeks," Bluethon said, "due to a catastrophic and unexpected side effect of our experiments in transference."

"Transference?"

"The instantaneous transfer of objects from one point to another," the woman clarified.

"Which your presence here has validated." The man's brief grin turned somber. "Although the circumstances are most unfortunate."

***

Forty minutes of Q &A left Jem seething. "Let me get this straight," she said, arms folded across her chest and glaring at the two doctors. "Your experiment goes wacko, blows up your lab, destroys a hanger and mail pod over *two frigging hundred kilometers away*...kills two people and drags me and piles of debris back to your lab. And you don't inform the authorities about any of it? Or me?"

She'd left her pocket contents sitting next to Dani's computer station so as not to lose them when hanging upside down over the pod. All of it must have been completely destroyed, too, otherwise the authorities would have posted her name and searched for her after finding either her ID or phone in the mess.

"Well, we did have to order new equipment and patch the hole in the wall," the man said, half apologetic. "So that's on record."

Jem shot him a dirty look. "But *I'm* not. You're keeping me here, basically hidden. If it was truly an accident, why all the frigging secrecy?" she demanded, her voice climbing. A tingling sensation flashed through her. *Now what?* Jem fumed. Her vision had gone wonky, with everything turning to various shades of gray and slightly fuzzy around the edges. Even the doctors.

Dr. Bluethon sighed. "Well, crap."

Dr. Lammstein scanned the room. "Think she's still here?"

"Huh?" Jem shot him a baffled look.

"The door hasn't flung open, so I'd say yes," Bluethon replied, reaching down to pull a large hand-held mirror from one of her leg pockets. She held it up, mirror side toward Jem. "I'd say this is was one good reason for secrecy. How do you look?"

Jem's brows drew down, not seeing whatever—wait. She leaned forward. It only reflected the bed. Where was she?

"In case you haven't figured it out," Bluethon said calmly. "You've gone invisible. You've been doing that, on and off, ever since your arrival in the middle of our test station's debris."

It has to be some kind of trick. She lunged off the bed and reached for the mirror. Her hand went right through it. *What the hell?* She stared at her hand. It *looked* normal, but... She tried again. After the third try, she stumbled back, trembling.

"Actually, we're not entirely sure what is happening to you," Dr. Lammstein said. "Now that you appear to have, uh, stabilized, we're hoping you can tell us."

Jem opened her mouth. Nothing came out. No words, no scream. No pain either, she belatedly realized, now or when she lunged off the bed. Her eyes darted around the room. Nothing but fuzzy grayness. Looking down, Jem found her right leg halfway *in* the bed. She shuddered and moved forward until her leg was free of it.

How do I get out of this?

"Don't panic, Miss Wilmont," Bluethon said blithely, glancing around the room.

Too frigging late!

"None of your...episodes have lasted long. About fifteen, twenty minutes at the most. We're not sure what triggers them. Although, going on what just happened, I'd say emotion is one possibility."

"I concur," Lammstein said. "Now that she's lucid, we can run tests. See how much control she can exercise over it and determine the extent of her DNA changes."

DN—oh, my, God. This is permanent?

Bluethon's tone turned brisk. "Right. Miss Wilmont? Let's try for a bit of control. Take deep breaths and relax."

That's frigging easy for you to say!

She did try relaxing, until she realized her chest wasn't expanding when she tried inhaling. In fact, her chest wasn't moving at all. Panic briefly set in. *But…if I'm not breathing, why haven't I passed out or died by now?*

"Doesn't appear to be working," Dr. Lammstein muttered.

Dr. Bluethon shot him a stern look. "Learning curve, Ric, and there's no manual. She's going to have to feel her way out of it."

Shit, damn, crap. I am so screwed.

***

"Your hand passed through the mirror?" Lammstein said, narrow-eyed. "You're sure?"

It'd taken another fifteen minutes or so for whatever it was to wear off, then she could talk again and her vision returned to normal. She'd spent twice that amount of time detailing what she'd experienced. Repeatedly. Jem shot him a sour look from her propped up position on the bed.

"How many times—"

"He's not being difficult, Miss Wilmont—may I call you Jem? It's the implication we are dealing with," Dr. Bluethon said gently. "Invisibility is apparently a side product of what you are actually experiencing, not the independent act itself that we had assumed it was."

"Unbelievable," the man muttered. "If that's what she is doing…it's unbelievable, Marion. Just…unbelievable."

"It has to be an adaptation of the Otanak field," she agreed, nodding.

"Otanak field?" Jem said sharply. "Are you crazy or suicidal?"

Everyone knew Otanak engines and gravity fields were an explosive mix. That's why standard ion engines were used to navigate a vessel out to a safely calculated low-to-no-gravity transition point before engaging them.

"Neither," Bluethon said, sounding slightly insulted. "We're only simulating fields *similar* to what the engines themselves generate and *only* on a small scale. And, apparently, so are you."

"Undoubtedly," Lammstein said, nodding. "But having a human manifesting a similar aspect of an Otanak field as an engine? Can a human body withstand that? For how long?"

Jem swallowed. That did not sound good.

The woman studied Jem for a moment. "You, my dear, are blurring the boundaries of reality. By some unknown, unbelievable process you are phasing out of our plane of existence. Our dimension, if you will. If I hadn't witnessed it firsthand…" she murmured, shaking her head. She continued with, "Physical objects here have no correlation with where you are. The two planes simply do not exist for each other, which is why your hand passed through the mirror."

"That explains how she's been getting out," Dr. Lammstein said.

"How much do you remember of these past weeks?" Dr. Bluethon asked.

"Bits and pieces, mostly. Nightmares, vertigo, pain." She adjusted her position slightly as the pain in her back had returned along with visibility.

"The best description for your mental state would have been 'delirious,' interspersed with bouts of…confusion."

"Interspersed with rounds of *puking*," Jem said sourly. That she definitely remembered.

"Your experience was probably more like a bad response to an illegal drug," Dr. Lammstein said, "Documented effects of various—"

Jem pressed her lips together to hide the grin when Bluethon interrupted with rolled eyes and a "Not relevant." The guy was the cerebral type, ready to launch a scientific lecture on any subject.

"Anyway," Bluethon continued, "there were times when you disappeared, not just visually, but out of your room. We'd finally find you somewhere outside. Our lab—Myerstone—and Christine's home—here—are in a relatively sparse rural area. Still, you didn't need to be wandering around, especially with thin clothes in January temps. Plus, there's both a deep pond and a ravine with a nasty drop-off in the area. It really worried us and we couldn't figure out how you were getting out, although," she grimaced, "we should have guessed something else was going on."

"She's been pretty lucky, so far…or is it instinctive?" Lammstein added thoughtfully.

"Ric?"

"The *phasing*, Marion. She could have exited it in the middle of a wall, an equipment rack, a tree, or even another person. No telling what the result would be like." He shrugged. "Probably messy."

Jem's horrified expression matched the woman's.

"Instinctive, then, I'd posit," he continued, tapping his chin. "After four weeks, the odds—" Marion smacked his arm. "What?"

"Never mind the odds." Marion glared at him for a few moments, then turned to Jem. Giving what she probably thought was an encouraging smile, she said, "Even though your frontal lobe wasn't fully cognizant of your…state, your hindbrain would have maintained situational awareness. That's the area responsible for autonomic functions, including balance and movement. Think reflex and instinct. Like grabbing for something when you trip or keeping your feet on a path while your thoughts are elsewhere."

Jem pursed her lips. That did *not* inspire confidence.

"I'm going with part instinct and part lobal cooperation. We have no idea what area of your brain controls this dimensional phasing, Jem, but they're obviously working together because Ric is right."

"Fascinating," he said, eyes lighting up. "I hadn't considered that aspect. What area of the brain could generate—*control* such an effect? The Pons, maybe?" he muttered. "Maybe…maybe. It coordinates the signal flow between…"

Marion gave another exasperated eye-roll as his muttering drifted into an unintelligent mumble. "Anyway, what's on your ankle is a tracking bracelet. Ric borrowed it from a doctor he knows who works in a psychiatric hospital. A signal from a remote controller dispenses a knockout drug—it took three tries to find one that affected your system. Did you always have a high tolerance to drugs or is it another—never mind." She made an exasperated gesture. "The remote also activates a locator beacon. We installed a sensor under your mattress that sounds an alarm whenever your weight leaves it.

"Whoever is on watch—we all take turns—immediately checks your room and activates the injector if you couldn't be found." She tapped her chin. "*Phasing* explains the time gap between when it's triggered and when the locator beacon finally goes active. That was another thing we couldn't figure out: how invisibility shielded it. In actuality, nothing happened because you and the tracker didn't exist on this plane."

"Until I, uh, pop back," Jem rubbed her forehead. Exists, not-exists— it was giving her a headache. "Then the bracelet receives the signal and activates both functions?"

"Yes. We'd head out as soon as the tracking signal pinged and, fortunately, you were never too far—usually less than half a kilometer. Although, once you did almost make it to the lab. That's about a kilometer to the east."

"You going to remove that sensor now?" Jem asked. "And the bracelet?"

"Ah, no," Lammstein said, his tone apologetic. "Not until we're sure there are no more reoccurring, ah, bouts of nightmare-fueled wanderings. You could be seriously injured."

Bluethon's smile was sympathetic, but she didn't contradict him.

Yeah, right. Find and clean up, if necessary. Yuck.

"At least no one's going to miss her," Dr. Lammstein added, absently.

"*Ric!*" Dr. Bluethon yelped as Jem shot him a withering glare.

"What? Oh. Sorry, that did sound bad," he apologized, coloring slightly. "What I meant was that we can deal with this situation quietly, and not have to make hasty decisions before…I mean…you know…" he trailed off helplessly.

"Yes, we get it," Dr. Bluethon snapped. "On that sour note, we're leaving."

Jem's brooding deepened as the woman ushered Dr. Lammstein out the door after wishing her a good day. A good day? Her life—*her*—had been permanently altered. *What do I do now? What if I can't control this? What happens if my brain gets in a snit-fit and the one area ignores the other one's direction?* That last question had her shuddering.

She stared at the band around her ankle. Was this her future? Shackled and tracked like, like some exotic creature? Is that how they saw her? Someone no longer completely human?

Were they right?

Jem stared unseeing at the door.

Chapter 3

Jem shuffled into the kitchen and carefully lowered herself into a chair. Since her 'awakening' eight days ago, the painful flareups along various nerve routes had been reduced to happening with an occasional wrong or sudden movement. The daily headaches were also gradually diminishing. The current throb in her temple was due to something else.

Angie McMillian, her babysitter for the day, bustled over and set a plate down in front of her. Jem eyed the long, pointed nails that somehow reminded her of claws.

"How you feeling?" Angie asked.

"Sore," she replied brusquely. Couldn't they start a conversation with something else? Although, she conceded grumpily, last night did give them a valid reason. And it wasn't as if she'd made things easy. Anger and resentment, her dominant emotions for the past week, made her conversational responses mostly brusque one-liners or silent glares.

Settling down opposite Jem with her own plate, Angie said, "Tonight's main course is fried duck."

Jem's eyes widened.

"Consider it revenge," Angie added with a grin.

"Seriously?" Jem poked at the golden-brown chunk of meat with a fork. She looked up on hearing Angie's laugh.

"No, it's chicken," the woman admitted. "But you can fantasize."

Jem grunted out a *ha, ha*, angrily stabbing her fork into the green beans. Yeah, they probably thought it was funny. But they weren't sporting a bunch of bruises. Those damn duck bills were *hard*. And as much as she disliked the constant monitoring, the doctors had been right about keeping the bracelet on. This time.

She'd come out of a nightmare on the edge of a pond last night. While still disorientated, the *shift* ended suddenly. Her bare feet had sunk into cold mud and a warning pinch in her ankle meant the injector had fired. She'd spent the next seconds of consciousness fighting off about a dozen ducks who evidently objected to her presence until she finally collapsed, gaining yet another bruise from banging her head on the hard ground.

They were still eating when Christine Blackburne barged through the door and collapsed into another chair. This being Christine's home, she was Jem's default nighttime sitter.

Christine gave a dramatic sigh. "Done, done, *done*. The last of the new equipment has finally been calibrated to Dr. L's satisfaction."

Angie pointed one of those claws at her. "Don't jinx it. Else he or Marion will find something else that needs 'adjusting.' Food is on the stove."

Jem found it interesting that while they always referred to Dr. Lammstein a bit formally, they all called Dr. Bluethon by her given name.

"True. But, as of when I left, Myerstone Lab is fully functional again."

"So, you going to ruin someone else's life now?" The accusation was out before Jem could stop it. Both women pinned her with stares in the thick silence.

Lips pressed into a hard line, Christine leaned on the tabletop. "We have apologized, repeatedly, for an *accident* that happened for *unknown reasons* since all our equipment was destroyed in said *accident*."

"And Dani and the courier's deaths? You'll just let those go on as unexplained?" Jem replied stubbornly. "Their families deserve better."

Dani had been her closest friend since high school, helping her through the gloomy clouds of Granny's passing two weeks after their graduation. She'd celebrated with Dani and funny, guitar-playing Samuel Torres when they fell in love and married. Then she'd held a weeping, devastated Dani at Sam's memorial nineteen months later.

"Do you think those deaths don't bother us? Well, think again," Christine said, voice dripping with anger. "Hell, I still wake up in a sweat. Especially after reliving that *wonderful* moment of getting slapped in the face with a severed hand."

Jem's stomach rolled, remembering how she'd slung Dani's hand away.

"We all regret, very much so, the deaths," Angie said quietly. "And what you've gone through—are going through still. Yes, we could have gone to the authorities and taken our lumps. That would have only made things worse for you."

"What do you think would've happened?" Mockingly, Christine answered her own question. "Besides making you a guinea pig for their scientists, just think of all the ways the authorities could use an invisible person."

Jem winced. Images of being poked and prodded, of slouching unseen through buildings or spying on meetings, careened past her mind's eye. And learning about her phasing? *"The ramifications of its capabilities are unprecedented,"* Dr. L had told her in a very serious voice, *"either for personal gain or so-called 'good intentions.'"* Which is why the doctors had cautioned her about not letting anyone else know the full extent of her mutation. Not even the other team members.

Jem's hostility bled away in the silence that followed. They had accepted responsibility for her. They had, and still were, protecting her. It was time she accepted that.

Christine blew out a breath and, evidently, most of her anger. "Besides, we couldn't do anything with you for a couple of hours while you popped in and out of visibility in the middle of that mess.”

“You were flickering like a neon sign in a bar window,” Angie interjected with a small grin.

Christine nodded. “By the time you became accessible, everyone’s shock had worn off and we weren’t sure what to do. By then, we’d seen the news report about the UPMS hanger and put the pieces together.” She winced. “Sorry, bad pun.”

“We held a meeting,” Angie said as Christine went to fill a plate. “We decided to, yes, hide you. The one stroke of luck was it happening late evening and the estate’s day workers had gone home. It gave us a chance to deal with,” she swallowed, “things. As your flickering episodes became spaced, we managed to get you here from the lab.”

“Made for some interesting moments,” Christine commented from the stove.

“True.” Angie snickered, then turned serious. “We looked after you best we could, although the damn flickering made some things nigh impossible.”

“Like an IV,” Jem said.

“Yeah. That would have been nice,” she said with a sigh. “Especially those first two weeks. Trying to feed you required coveralls, a bucket, and good reflexes.”

Jem’s checks colored slightly. “Sorry?”

“Luck came in handy, too, and not just at feeding time,” Christine said, regaining her seat. Her plate was piled high with vegetables but no meat. “Like the day Marion leaned over the bed to examine you. She was wearing a loose blouse and you shot a no-notice volley all the way down her torso…underneath it.”

Mortified, Jem’s whole face went red as Angie valiantly tried to hold back a grin.

“At least she wasn’t wearing a bra that day,” Christine continued, waving a green-bean-impaled fork. "Let me tell you, having a bra full of squishy stuff coating your boobs is the definition of *yuck*. Wipe that horrified look off, Jem. My experience came courtesy of a two-year-old nephew and an ill-timed hug."

Giggling, Angie pushed her empty plate aside. "The doctors have tabled any new test runs until we have an idea of what happened and why. We've spent the past month pulling together our notes—including emailed memos we sent to each other—along with our recollections to try and figure it out. Fortunately, our main research had been backed up to a separate server in the main house so we have a starting point."

"Have you made any progress with your invisibility?" Christine asked.

Jem poked at the last of her chicken. "No, not really. I can recognize the…tingle?...that tells me it's happening. But controlling it? Starting it, much less stopping it? How do I wrangle the impossible?"

The women's sympathetic smiles didn't provide an answer.

***

Weeks passed, and her determination to make the best of things was offset with bouts of anger, resentment, depression, and even fatalism. Days when she felt as dead as Dani. Days when she wished she was, especially during episodes of uncontrolled bar-sign flickering. Nights she was afraid to sleep, terrified of where or how she'd awaken. The lab team did their best to buoy Jem's spirits as she struggled with her new reality.

Jem was flabbergasted to learn Ruben Davis, who loved to wear a red bulb nose and crack the worst jokes, was considered one of Earth's top theoretical physicists. Jonnie Sinclair's eidetic memory included every card game and trick invented. Angie McMillian's mood was reflected in her hair color, both subject to rapid change. Lee Ybarra often had a parrot on his shoulder—a frigging real bird—and it was a toss-up on which one had the dirtiest mouth. Christine Blackburne's cupcakes and cookies were decadent late-night snacks enjoyed over idle conversation. Dr. Bluethon was the mother hen to them all, and Jem soon found herself calling her Marion, too. Dr. L was the quintessential scientist…beyond brilliant in some ways and totally clueless in others.

Neal Grathen was her least favorite of the team. She didn't know if it was his loud, odd-colored shirts with tacky sayings on them or his general air of distain. Or maybe it was because he had never made her feel welcome, more like an odious chore he couldn't get out of.

She also learned more about what had happened, at least the basics. Marion had translated parts of it into non-genius for her, but a lot of it still zipped right past her. Saying they were cutting new paths in quantum physics and dimensional mechanics was an understatement.

It had been their third full-powered test. Like the first two, nothing was happening to the block of wood sitting in the primary test station, which was located a couple of meters behind the lab. The wood didn't transfer, didn't so much as wiggle. *Living up to its reputation*, Ruben had joked. They began making random adjustments to both the primary and secondary's various inputs. Jonnie remembered making an adjustment to the primary's electromagnetic field when his instruments redlined and everything went haywire: smoking, arcing equipment, and loud explosions.

All they knew for certain was that there was a major power surge combined with a wildly fluctuating, out-of-control Otanak field. Which came first, which was the cause or the effect, was unknown due to the immediate loss of equipment—Angie's rather spectacularly, leaving her with singed eyebrows and a slightly-toasted face. A coupler on the power generator exploded; so did the primary station. Then they found Jem in the primary's wreckage, as well as debris from the hanger and the secondary site, which was about a hundred meters away in a field. What had felt like forever to her in that black hell had actually lasted only seconds.

They theorized she survived due to being inside the mail pod and right next to its O-engine. However, they were stumped about her changes. Nothing they could think of, even theorize about, would account for DNA mutation. After one frustratingly no-progress meeting, Marion had thrown up her hands in frustration, declaring "People have been traveling by Otanak drive for several centuries now without adverse effects, for Pete's sake. Even those taking the fast route in a UPSM courier pod."

While the lab team worked hard on figuring out all the esoteric stuff, Jem worked just as hard on *shifting*. Finally, halfway through the third month AB—'After Boom' as they'd taken to calling it—she successfully stopped a *shift* from happening. After a couple of more weeks, she was successfully controlling her switch to invisibility, which put an end to the flickering. She still had to wait out the fifteen or so minutes it took for it to run its course, but vowed she'd get that, too.

They threw a small party to celebrate at Christine's. Her happy bubble was ruptured the next morning by an orange shirt with chartreuse windmills and its obnoxious owner.

"So, given any thought to future plans?"

Christine had left for the lab shortly after Neal Grathen had shown up. Arm thrown casually across the chair back, his derisive tone had Jem pursing her lips. "No," she replied, ignoring everything below his neck.

"Not too many career paths for a talent like yours," he said.

Jem did not like the crafty look in his eyes or his tone. She set down her fork and leaned back. "I have no intention of spying or stealing, if that's what you're insinuating."

"Just making an observation."

Uh-huh. "Well, your *observation* needs glasses," Jem said tartly.

"You think the others haven't thought the same?" he snapped. "Ever wondered why you're still wearing that tracker?"

Her shoulders stiffened. Dr. L had waffled last night when she'd asked him to remove it. After all, it wasn't needed now that she could control going into a phased shift. He had agreed to leave the drug injector empty. Finally. Knowing she could be knocked unconscious on someone's whim was both irritating and worrisome.

Neal straightened. "Your *intentions* now may not be the same tomorrow. Or next month. Or after you leave here." His tone altered from testy to sarcastic. "And they won't be worth a damn when others learn what you can do."

The small ember of disquiet she'd been ignoring flared into life. Jem knew he was right, and the jerk only knew about the invisibility. No longer hungry, she rose and dumped her breakfast remains in the trash. Rinsed her plate off in the sink as her thoughts turned brutally honest. Would the temptation to do whatever she wanted prove to be too much? Be forced into doing something awful by an asshole who learned her secret? *And how far will I go, what will I be willing to do, to protect my secrets…or protect others from them?*

A tremor worked its way down her spine.

Jem went into the living room and plopped down on the couch opposite the viewscreen. From the movie menu, she selected *Clue*, an old twentieth-century favorite. Maybe a fun, light-hearted movie filled with double entendre could get her mind off her not-so-light-hearted life. She settled back as the opening credits splashed across the screen.

Unfortunately, by the time Wadsworth was parking in front of the forbidding-looking mansion, her attention was already wandering. No, she couldn't blame the team for worrying. The only way to minimize all of their fears was gaining full control over this shifting crap. Which meant stopping it on command as well as starting it.

Jem only half-noted the character throwing chunks of meaty bones to the two dogs, but had to grin as he glared at them after realizing he'd stepped in their 'gift' to him. *Dogs will be dogs.*

She blew out a breath. Okay, how to stop a *shift* in its track? There had to be some way to consciously cut it off. After all, the tug-like feeling she felt right before it terminated had to be connected, kinda-sorta, to something in her brain. She needed to find that switch.

Jem snorted out a laugh when Wadsworth yelled for the dog to sit, but it was Mr. Green's butt hitting the bench. Her amusement faded. Hadn't she been the obedient one? Always acquiescing with whatever Dr. L and Marion wanted? Well, screw that. As messed up as it was, this was her life. From now on, she'd be proactive. Jem glanced toward the kitchen; her lip curled. No more babysitters.

***

"That is just…creepy," Angie said around the spoon in her mouth. Christine had declared tonight as girl's night, and the four of them were sitting around her living room with single-serving canisters of ice cream.

It had been two weeks since she'd won the no-babysitting argument, and she'd spent her solitary days practicing. While she still couldn't deliberately end it, she'd learned to vary a *shift's* intensity. Tonight had been a good excuse to show off. Jem spent several minutes, 'fading' herself from transparent to opaque to complete invisibility and back to transparent.

"It's like you're a ghost," Christine said, slightly awed.

Jem gave a thumbs-up reply.

"So, once it's engaged, you can dial it—so to speak—from slightly there to complete invisibility," Marion said, eyes narrowed in concentration.

Jem shook her head. The woman just couldn't put the scientist aside.

"Spooky, yeah, but at least you can still semi-communicate this way," Christine said. "Sign language, pointing, etcetera."

Marion set her ice cream down. "Have you tried reversing all the way out?" The serious tone had the other two women straightening and looking hopeful.

Jem nodded, and spread her arms in an unmistakable frustrated gesture. *Of course I tried.*

"Well, damn," Marion said, sighing.

It was another ten minutes before Jem 'rejoined' them. Tired, she plopped down in her chair and picked up her tub of half-melted cherry-vanilla ice cream. The others had pretty much finished theirs.

"I've tried," Jem said, able now to vent her frustration. "Sometimes it seems as if I can almost make it back or out of, of—have you ever come up with a name for it?"

"We're still discussing it," Marion replied, shooting Christine an annoyed look.

"There is nothing wrong with *chameling,*" Christine said, waving her spoon. "Jem is a chameleon. Just like that lizard that can make itself invisible."

Angie snorted. "*Chameling* also beats those eight syllable things you and Dr. L are batting back and forth."

"What's wrong with just plain *shifting*?" Jem said, exasperated. "I know, let's call it *poofing.*"

The expression on Marion's face had all three of them laughing.

Marion rolled her eyes. "None of those are *scientifically* descriptive or acceptable. We don't want to use some derivative of the Otanak fields because we don't believe that's accurate. The conditions you've shared—from lack of breathing and heartbeat to visual and audio impairment—are indications you're experiencing a true stasis state. That aligns more with the theoretical suppositions of an interdimensional boundary's state, which is a non-physical, non-everything hypothetical divide separating the true physical dimensions. Keeps them from overlapping or intersecting, both of which, theoretically, wouldn't be good."

Jem gave her a blank, slightly glazed look.

"Oh, crap," Marion added ruefully, seeing Christine and Angie's wide-eyed stares.

"*Lack* of breathing and heartbeat?" Angie repeated.

"Interdimensional boundary's state? That means Jem is going completely out of *our* dimension, Marion," Christine accused angrily.

"How long have you known that?" Angie asked, her unhappy tone brusque.

Marion sighed. "Obviously, Ric and I have known since we could hold a coherent conversation with Jem. And before your knickers get twisted, we asked Jem not to say anything about it. *Becaaaause*," Marion drawled, cutting Christine off, "if you think people will flip out over invisibility, think what knowledge of someone capable of an interdimensional stasis would do."

Christine and Angie both acquired thoughtful looks.

"For that reason, Ric and I felt it needed to be kept as limited as possible. I would appreciate it if you two would consider her phased stasis as privileged information," Marion finished, giving Jem a veiled look.

She understood. By stressing it as only a 'stasis' condition, Marion was still hiding the *phasing's* full capability.

The tense silence lasted for about a minute before Christine broke it.

"Well, then, that answers what to call it. Phasing. Simple, yet accurate."

Marion shook her head. "We've been avoiding that term for obvious reasons. It could engender all kinds of questions, especially from those we'd rather not be asking them."

"Not if we say she's sliding—*phasing*—along the electromagnetic spectrum and out of the human detectable wavelengths," Christine offered.

Marion's lips pursed. "That's…a very good idea."

"Does that mean she'd never die if she failed to fully come back out of a dimensional shift?" Angie asked, forehead furrowed in concern.

Jem's spoon froze halfway in horror. A non-existent existence? Unable to interact with others? *Forever?*

"What would happen if she punched through—for lack of a better term—that boundary into a different dimension than ours?" Christine asked Marion in a thoughtful voice. "Does that become her new reality—assuming she can survive there? Can she return via the same method back to this one?"

"Hmmm, good questions," Marion said, her gaze unfocused in contemplation.

Jem cleared her throat. "Guys, you are creeping *me* out. This was supposed to be a fun evening, not an outline for a scientific thesis. A horrific one at that," she muttered.

"Agreed." Christine flashed a smile. "We don't need to be weirding ourselves out."

"True. But the questions are potentially more than hypothetical, considering what we do and do not know about—"

"Marion, chill!" Angie said, waving her hands. "Theorize tomorrow. Tonight is for food, drink, and *trying* for normalcy."

The conversation drifted, the subjects kept mundane and non-scientific. A pang of sorrow briefly hit Jem, remembering similar evenings she'd passed with Dani. Eventually it wound back around to her and how she was doing. Jem saw her opening.

"I'm doing okay—adapting," Jem said, turning toward Marion. "Which is why I don't feel the need for a tracker anymore." Losing that argument a second time with Dr. L two days ago had grated. "I've proven I can control a *shift's* start—not being able to stop it, yet, is immaterial."

Marion hesitated. "Ric is worried about any new effects suddenly cropping up."

"Is he? Are you?" Jem said, running a narrow-eyed gaze over her listeners. "The way I hear it, you're worried that I'd take off and utilize my…ability in a questionable manner."

Marion's lips pursed while Angie and Christine exchanged looks. "Where did you hear that?"

"Grathen."

"Oh, him."

"He's an asshole," Angie said over Christine's derisive mutter. "He enjoys throwing his weight around."

"Is he still bothering you?" Marion asked, giving Angie a sharp look. "Ric specifically told him to leave you alone. Said that if he didn't know what 'no' meant, his next employer could explain it."

Angie waved a hand. "It's down to squinty-eyed glares and cold shoulders, all of which I ignore."

Marion drummed her fingers on her thigh. "Neal's an excellent technician, but we can always bring in someone new—brief them on the data and situation." She flashed a smile at Jem. "With a few exceptions, of course. Maybe we should just go ahead and let him go."

"That might not be wise," Jem said, remembering the kitchen confrontation. "How well do you trust him to not disclose what's happened?"

"Not even a bit," Christine said flatly. "Angie's not the only one that's experienced that spiteful streak of his, and I don't believe our contract stipulations mean a damn thing to him. Seriously. He'll be telling Law Enforcement everything about the hanger explosion as soon as he's out the door. Following right behind it will be everything about Jem to whoever will pay him the most for it." She stabbed a finger at Marion. "And that right there validates your and Dr. L's decision to keep the full knowledge of it limited."

Marion's mouth opened, closed as Angie's head bobbed vigorously in agreement. Worry lines appeared on her forehead.

"You and Dr. L would be hard-pressed to sue him or do anything about it when you're fighting LE yourselves. As for Jem…" they all looked over at her, "…no telling what will happen to her," Angie finished.

"Well, shit," Marion said, rubbing her neck. "Alright, we're stuck with him—for now. Ric and I will keep a closer eye on him." Her steady gaze met Jem's. "I've gotten to know you fairly well, these past few months. Neither Ric nor I believe you're going to go rogue and turn to criminal activities. More importantly, you're not only stable, you're *sane*."

Jem's mouth dropped open. Despite all the emotional turbulence she'd gone through, that had never occurred to her.

"That's right," Marion said, nodding. "We were worried that your experiences, both the initial trauma and the ongoing effects, would lead to mental degradation."

"Insanity," Jem replied flatly. Or worse: a brain-dead vegetable. "Is it still possible?"

"The human brain, even today, is a mysterious place," Marion replied gently. "There is still so much we don't understand. There's no telling what long-term effects phasing will cause. Anything, I'm afraid, is possible."

"Developing mental issues is something everyone faces, Jem," Angie said. "There's still no cure for dementia or schizophrenia or other diagnoses." She paused, took a breath. "My own grandmother went legally insane three years ago."

From the others' registered shock, that was news to all of them.

"Oh, Angie. Why didn't you say something?" Christine asked.

Angie shrugged. "Kind of hard to work that into a conversation."

Shaking her head, Marion turned back to Jem. "What I said applies physically, too. Your *phasing* is being powered by you—your body's energy. Unlike an externally powered Otanak engine, you don't have an unlimited supply. That's why it eventually fails, you 'fall back', and have to 'recharge' before you can *phase* again. The stop-restart sequence has to have some effect on your internal organs.”

Jem slumped down in her seat. That explained her tiredness. “Any other good news?” she muttered.

“I think that should cover it,” Christine said, concern scrunching her brows.

“Regardless,” Marion waved a hand, “here and now, our current worry is the possibility of manipulation and/or extortion by others. You’ll have to be extremely careful of who you can trust.”

“That’s a given,” Jem said with quiet resignation. A lifetime of looking over her shoulder, guarding herself. Watching for signs of mental and organ *degradation*. Lovely.

“Speaking of which…” Marion’s lips turned up in a rueful smile, “trust must go both ways. How can you trust us if we don’t trust you? I agree; it’s time the anklet came off.”

“We’ll drink to that,” Christine and Angie chorused, holding up their drinks.

Chapter 4

"What happened?" Marion demanded as she barreled into the kitchen. Christine was hard on her heels.

Jem raised her head from her arms and gave them a bleary smile. "I found your gully." She'd managed to drag herself back to the house, then used Christine's table comp to call the lab before collapsing into a kitchen chair.

Marion raised Jem's chin, examining her eyes before carefully lifting a lock of her hair to study her forehead. "That's a nasty looking gash. Did you lose consciousness?"

"Briefly." Jem blinked. "And it's kind of hard to focus."

"Concussion," Christine said, plopping a bag down on the table that Jem knew held medical supplies. She and Marion both had medical training in their resumes, which was another reason they had decided to take care of her themselves when there were no obvious physical injuries.

Jem flinched when Marion ran her hand through her hair.

"Large hematoma above right ear," Marion called out, gently separating hair strands for a better look.

Jem flinched again.

"Sensitivity along right ribcage," Christine said, pulling up Jem's shirt. "Wow. Bruising's already started. Any movement—does it feel like something's broken? Hard to breathe?"

"No, I don't think I landed hard enough for that," Jem said, wincing as Christine gently ran her fingers over very sore ribs.

"Okay, explain," Marion ordered, starting to swab Jem's forehead.

"Not much to it," Jem replied, closing her eyes. "I went for a walk—found the gully. I was looking down into it when the edge crumbled beneath my feet." It was mostly true.

Yes, she'd gone for a walk, but while *shifted*. She'd been practicing—playing, she admitted honestly. Maybe she had gotten a bit exuberant after the tracker was removed last week. She'd *phased* through trees and bushes and even swiped her hand through a couple of large rocks. On arriving at the ravine, she'd 'stepped out' over it after noting that she had 'walked' over several dips in her path. Evidently her *phased* body ignored the 'real' terrain. Instead of marveling about literally walking on air, she should have been keeping track of the time. The end-of-shift tug had come abruptly, with the obvious result.

She'd come to at the bottom of the ravine.

"Need to get a new phone," Jem told them, wincing as Marion applied an ointment to her forehead. "Not sure how long it took to make it back here." This was one instance having the tracker on would have been welcome. Even if it meant laying there until they found her.

"Ribs bruised…maybe a hairline fracture," Christine announced with a frown. "I'll wrap her after you finish. "See a number of other bruises—about to be expected after communing with rocks."

"Alright, the gash was more blood than depth, so no stitches. Hold off on the wrapping until after she's showered off all the dirt." Marion stepped back, put hands on hips. "Christine will stay with you. I have to get back and help Ric deal with an annoying person that's been pestering us."

"Once she's finished wrapping me, it's not necessary—"

"Oh, yes, it is," Marion interrupted. "You've a concussion—mild right now. But other symptoms can manifest later. And that's on top of the physical injuries you'll need help with. And no *phasing*," she ordered, wagging a finger. "No telling how your brain will react."

Jem already knew how. Rather, how it didn't. She'd tried to take the painless route back here. Nada, zilch. Evidently pain neurons short-circuited her shifting ones.

"There's even the possibility of latent hemorrhaging," Marion continued sternly. "So, suck it up, Jem. For the next…*mmm*…week at least, babysitting is back on the work schedule."

Well, phooey.

***

Jem had to admit the women had been right. She'd managed to shower by herself, but a dizzy spell had hit while Christine was wrapping her ribs. A minor one, compared to her previous bouts of post-AB vertigo. Still, she'd welcomed Christine's help in getting from bathroom to bedroom and dressing. She settled back against the pillows.

Well, crap, Jem thought, running a finger over her bandaged forehead. She'd planned on talking with Marion. With the ability to control a shift's start, there was no longer a reason for her to remain here. *Was*, is right, she grumped. She'd certainly fouled that up.

"You must have dropped like a rock," Christine remarked, tugging a blanket around Jem's waist. "If you'd tumbled down it, the damage would have been all over, instead of mostly just on your right side."

"Yep, went straight down," Jem said. That certainly wasn't a lie.

"I'll get you something to wash down a couple of pain pills. Head has to be pounding."

"Tea, if you don't mind. And, yeah, it is. Ribs are complaining, too."

"Don't doubt it. Want something to snack on, too?"

Jem perked up. "Got any cupcakes hidden?"

Christine chuckled. "No, but I can whip up a batch. Sorry you're hurt, but thank you for giving me a reason to stay here."

"Oh? Who's the annoying pest?" Jem asked, remembering Marion's remark.

Christine grimaced. "Reginald Kurzvall. He's a super-mega-rich industrialist who just happens to be Myerstone's primary funding source. Guess he feels his credits buy him the right to dictate what we do. Now that both test stations have been rebuilt and the lab is functional again, he's been hounding us to restart experiments."

Jem's eyes widened.

Christine patted her leg. "Don't worry. Dr. L and Marion aren't about to restart things until we have a better understanding of what went wrong last time. They've determined that the secondary station must have switched from receiver to either an amplifier or relay—still TBD why— and then the field latched on to the first O-engine in a direct line with the two test stations."

"And me."

"And you. Murphy's Law and its addendum in action: not only did it go wrong, it happened at the worst possible time."

"Sounds like it's striking again with this Kruzville."

"Kurzvall," Christine corrected, "and you might be right. Mr. Mega-credits lives on Hermes Four. He deliberately blindsided us this morning, showing up without warning to personally state his demands since we weren't," she did the air quote thingy, "taking his messages seriously enough."

"Is he aware of, ah, everything that happened? Of me?"

"Hell, no. Only about all the lab damages." She frowned. "To be honest, from the impression I got, I don't think it would've mattered to him. He'd probably view your experience as proof that our theories worked."

"At the cost of two lives." Jem replied sharply.

"So we just need to work the bugs out." She held up a hand at Jem's angry expression. "Which we will do and why we are standing firm on no new transference experiments for now. None of us wants a repeat of what happened to you and those two unfortunates."

She bustled out, returning with a glass of tea and two pills.

Jem accepted them, then fixed on her with a serious look. "Christine, I haven't told you how much I appreciate all you're doing for me. Putting up with me, even when I'm a noxious pain. Sharing your home."

"You have the Universe's right to be as big as a pain as you want to be," she said, her tone as serious as Jem's gaze. "Considering why you're here and that we're the reason for it, it's the least we can do. It may have started as an obligation, Jem, but I've come to respect you and the way you've handled—make that adapted, to everything." Christine flashed a bright smile. "I'd like to think we're friends now."

Warmth spreading, Jem returned the smile and replied softly, "Friends."

"Good. Now that's settled, yell if you get to feeling bad," she told Jem, leaving the door open behind her.

Jem leaned her throbbing head back and mentally urged the pills to work faster.

***

"It's been almost four weeks. I'm healed. It's time to regain my life." Marion and Dr. L had shown up remarkedly fast after Christine informed them she was leaving.

"There could still be side-effects we don't know about," Dr. L protested. "After all, you still don't have full control. You can't stop the phasing once it's started."

"So? That simply means I won't be able to do anything until it wears off. What matters is that I *can* control when and where it starts. Then I only need to ensure I'm somewhere safely hidden when it's done."

"We understand, Jem. You want some semblance of a normal life," Marion said gently. "But, to be blunt, you aren't normal. Not any longer.

There is so much to consider now."

Jem's mouth set in a hard line. "So I'm a freak?"

"*No!*" they said forcefully and in tandem.

"Your condition is the result of converging circumstances and your own unique physicality," Marion continued strenuously. "Please, just give us a few more months. Please?"

Dr. L snapped his fingers. "Ned."

Both women gave him a questioning look.

"He asked me to hire summer help. I forgot about it," he said, a bit sheepishly.

"Perfect compromise," Marion said, beaming. "Room and board plus wages. You can work; we can monitor."

Jem eyed the two doctors as she considered it. She wanted to put the lab and all it represented behind her. True, she was a bit worried about that unknown part herself. A couple of months? Okay, she could do that.

"Alright," Jem said firmly, arms crossed. "Three months at the most. If no issues by then, I'm gone. In the meantime, I need to retrieve my stuff before it gets auctioned off."

***

Christine drove Jem into town the next morning. She purchased a new cash card and then loaded it with credits from her bank account. After giving the female Law Enforcer behind the desk a—somewhat—convincing story about losing her identification card in the pond after being attacked by ducks, she got a new one. The officer had taken a new picture, even though Jem still looked a lot like her eighteen-year-old self.

When she went to claim her travel bag, the bored clerk at the bus station didn't ask any question other than "*ID?*" and then stated the fee required to get it. Jem paid it, although she couldn't help wondering if the clerk had given himself a tip.

Then they did a bit of shopping and browsing before heading back to

Christine's house. Her new phone was paid for by Dr. L via Christine. According to her, he'd insisted. Perhaps as a small act of atonement on his part?

Chapter 5

The sun was still stretching its solar shoulders above the horizon when Christine drove them up the private lane. The estate had been purchased by the Myerstone Group, the foundation Dr. L and Marion had established. The hundred-plus acres gave privacy for their experimentation and the terrain they'd needed for the planned test stations. Set a short distance from the main road, the two-story house served as research facility, offices, conference room, and living quarters for most of the team members. A small non-scientific staff performed cleaning, cooking, yardwork, and general maintenance.

The driveway wound around the front of the house to a graveled parking area behind the attached three-car garage. Christine parked her Hydra Rover sedan between a well-used work truck and a Strato200 two-door Jem recognized as Jonnie's. Jem studied the innocent-looking building that sat another ten meters or so away, hidden from the road by the house's bulk. The lab must have started out as a large maintenance or storage building of some kind. She saw no windows and it had a wider-than-normal entrance protected by a narrow overhead cover. A newer, smaller shed sat a short distance off to the side.

They climbed out of the car.

"I know, it doesn't look like much." Christine waved her hand in its general direction. "But the lab itself is mostly for actual tests and such. We expanded it—the new section is in back for all the electrical lines and power stuff. Totally isolated from the main house."

Jem gave her a wry look over the car's hood. "Prudent, considering events."

Christine ignored that. "The conference room in the house is where we do a lot of the brainstorming and research. Come on, I'll introduce you."

Jem followed her into the garage, past the doctors' two vehicles, and into a well-appointed kitchen. An older couple sat at a small dining table in a corner nook. The woman's cup halted in mid-air.

"Christine. Don't usually see you here this early," she said.

"Yeah, well, you two start your days early so I needed to get Jem here." Both turned their attention to Jem. "Jem, this is Janet Espinoza Murphy and Ned Danford Kise, the husband-wife team that keeps us fed and this place running smoothly. Janet, Ned, meet Jem Seaborne Wilmont."

"Nice to meet you," the woman said politely.

Silence. The older couple looked between the two of them. Waiting.

Christine huffed out a breath. "Dr. L didn't tell you about her, did he?"

Ned's lips quirked. "No."

"Jem is a friend of mine that he's hired to help out for the summer. You told him you'd need help once things warmed up."

"Aye. That was three weeks ago. Figured he forgot. I was debatin' to remind him or just go at it myself." His gaze swept across Jem. "No offense, Miss Wilmont, but I need someone who can do a day's hard work."

Yes, she was on the skinny side of slender. But she'd put weight back on and, while her muscles hadn't had a decent workout lately, they hadn't deteriorated either.

Jem studied the older man in turn. Late fifties, maybe early sixties.

Hard to tell with his weathered features. Yard work and other maintenance activities probably didn't come as easy to him anymore. Despite available machinery, some things still required hands and knees.

"No offense taken, sir, and I'm stronger than I look. I've worked at general labor for six, seven years in everything from shoveling stables to waitressing. Even handled nets on a fishing trawler once." His eyebrows jerked up. Yeah, those nets were bulky and heavy, hard to manipulate. "However, I'm not mechanically inclined and can only do basic machine maintenance. Like oil and lube," she added with a smile.

"In that case," he said, "have a seat. Coffee? Takes at least two cups to charge my battery."

The woman snorted. "Get you a cup, too, Christine?" she asked, rising as Jem did as told.

"Thanks, but no. I'm going to go roll Angie out of bed. If I'm up, she can darn well be up too. Besides, we have research to do. Talk to you later, Jem." With a wave of her hand, Christine vanished down a hallway.

Jem waited silently, sipping her coffee while the two of them exchanged one of those wordless-speaking looks long-time partners developed. She idly wondered if anyone had done research to see if telepathy was possible.

"Sounds like you've a wanderin' foot," Ned said, taking a sip.

"Yes, sir. Granny died shortly after I graduated from public school. After settling her estate, I decided to see what I could of the world." She flashed a smile. "It's an amazing place that's managed to preserve much of its uniqueness."

"Your grandmother raised you?" Janet asked, her words holding curiosity.

"Great-grandmother. My parents died in a shuttle crash when I was thirteen. My father's people live on Magellan—Venice Two. There was on one else, so she took me in."

The woman nodded. "You'd already been uprooted enough. Sorry to hear of your losses. I've never met anyone with one eye brown and the other green."

Jem's lips quirked upward. "I've learned to ignore the double-takes."

"Were you promised room and board?"

"Yes, ma'am. My bag is in the car."

"Have you had breakfast?"

"Yes, ma'am."

Ned re-entered the conversation with "Will that long braid be a problem?" It hung almost to her belly button.

Jem shook her head. "I have clips to put it up if need be, especially around machinery."

Ned pushed away from the table. "Well, then, looks like you came dressed for work. Why don't you grab your bag and Janet will show you where to toss it." His wife rolled her eyes. "Then come on out to the shed and we'll get started."

***

The first hour was spent getting familiar with equipment and where-all the what-all was stored. By lunchtime, Jem's clothes were dirty, her pants sported a couple of grease streaks, and she couldn't be happier. Well, not counting the one thing she couldn't change. Dr. L wandered in as she was finishing her second chicken salad sandwich. Janet had served the team's lunch of sandwiches, chips, fruit, and tea before joining them in the kitchen.

"Can I get you anything else?" Janet asked, rising.

"No, no," he said, waving her back down. "Everything tastes great, as usual. I wanted to see how things are going. With Jem. I mean, is she working out okay?"

Ned didn't roll his eyes, but Jem was sure he wanted to.

"She's workin' just fine, Dr. Lammstein. Hired at the right time, too.

There's three flats of Begonias and Impatiens comin' that'll need be planted around the front."

Jem's nose crinkled. That deep tub in her bathroom would definitely be needed after a day bent over planting.

"Not to worry, Jem," Ned added, evidently seeing her reaction. "I've knee pads you can borrow."

Dr. Lammstein said, "Good. Good. Don't want any miscalculations to offset the current status quo." He ambled back out.

Jem stared after him, bemused. Was that a fancy way of referring to problems?

"Don't mind the doctor," Janet said, smiling. "He's a genius, intellectually, but a bit…vague on the personality side."

Ned snorted. "A bit short on common sense, too."

"Christine told me a bit about him and the others," Jem said, maintaining the pretense of having just met the other team members. "Said he and the other doctor—Bluethon?—were geniuses."

"Did she tell you about their 'miscalculation' several months back?" Ned asked, letting out a derisive snort. "The one that blew a three-meter hole in the lab wall?"

Jem stared. "There was mention of a hole, but—three meters?" *That's a bit more than 'patch up a hole,' Doc.*

"They overtaxed the lab's power generator," Janet confirmed, nodding.

An excellent cover story.

"It's a good thing they kept the lab completely separate from the house," Ned said, "as it shorted out every piece of electrical equipment in the buildin'. The two test stations they set up for experiments were destroyed—literally." He frowned down at his tea. "Shorted out and melted components, I understand. But blown into pieces, especially the one set a ways off in a field, doesn't make sense, and they've never explained it."

It bothered him, Jem realized. She sipped her tea in the ensuing silence. "Well," she finally said, "they fire the generator up, I'll be sure to stay away from the lab."

"You and us both," Ned agreed solemnly. "Their new one generates almost twice the power the last one did."

Jem's eyes widened.

Chapter 6

June and July passed quietly. Mostly. The team's voices could get loud as they debated and argued over theories and ideas for going forward. Occasionally, they'd do a low-power run with the lab generator to obtain different types of energy readings to bolster one theorem or another. They were energized at having their basic theories proved correct, albeit in an unfortunate manner. Jonnie, Jem observed with amusement, liked to express himself with arm movements. The louder he got, the wilder they got. She waited for the day he took off, like his parrot.

Jem spent her days either working with Ned outside or helping Janet inside. Once a week, she dusted and cleaned the lab building. In the evenings, after Ned and Janet left, they could mingle more easily—cards being the favorite pastime. That and debating. She sat in on one of their debates…for about half an hour. That's all it took for her brain to glaze over. She'd swear it was in an entirely different language. Sometimes she'd read or watch a program in her room or go home with Christine. They'd spend the evening eating decadent desserts while chatting or watching movies.

Other times, she'd just wander around the property. She'd loiter in the woods, watching and listening to their myriad of small critters. Or stand silent at the small, unmarked grave that held Dani's hand and the lower half of Justin Kelcie's right leg. She loved to watch the sky gradually fade through twilight into darkness. And the stars, so bright here away from city lights.

Things changed the last week of July.

Jem was getting a late evening snack in the kitchen when Neal Grathen stormed in, swearing unabatedly as he stomped down the hallway and up the stairs, undoubtedly heading for his room. Lips pursed, she watched the others come through the door with glum faces. All but Christine, who had gone home as usual.

"I'll call Symthe Security in the morning," Marion was saying.

"Why? All they can do is wipe the system," Ruben said sourly. "I can do that myself."

Uh-oh. Sounds like a major problem.

"Wiping the lab server means losing yesterday's data readings," Angie said. "Unless they've been copied to the backup server here?" she said, looking at the doctors hopefully. Her face fell when Marion shook her head. "Well, shit," she grumbled before making her way down the hallway.

"What happened?" Jem asked, a tad bit worried.

"We went out to do a low-level run to test how the Otanak energy fields interact with—never mind. I, uh, forgot we'd changed the code yesterday and entered the old one," Dr. L replied.

"Twice," Marion said, annoyance lacing her words, "which is why it locked up."

Oops. "Doesn't your security service have a reset code of some sort?"

Marion shook her head. "Only for the house. We set the lab's system up ourselves so it'd be completely independent—standalone, to avoid any possibility of hacking."

"I put one in when I built the new server," Ruben said, "but it's not working. Right now, the system will only accept input from the main panel inside. I hope. Except no one can get in." He rubbed his hands across his face.

Jem sympathized. Ruben and Christine were their IT experts, so she wasn't surprised he'd be taking the snafu personally. Christine certainly would when she found out.

Jonnie threw an arm across his sig-ner's shoulders. "Come on, Rube. Let's go watch a movie. Relax. You can put that brain to figuring out the glitch tomorrow." Both men waved a sad-faced good-night.

The two men had never been at Christine's at the same time, so Jem hadn't realized they were significant partners until after she moved to the main house.

"Ruben's wrong," Dr. L suddenly said. "Jem can get us in."

Marion shot a quick look down the hallway. "Keep your voice down," she warned in a low voice.

"What about the others? They'll realize there's more to me if I do," Jem said. They'd been adamant about keeping the full extent of her ability a secret.

"We'll lie," Marion said succinctly. Jem snorted.

"Will you help us?" Dr. L asked, his tone serious. "We can't afford to lose that data. Jonnie postulated a theory that we really need to verify."

Did they think she wouldn't? "Of course."

They went out to the lab, going around to the door in back. Twilight still lingered in the long mid-summer night and they didn't want anyone witnessing Jem's *phasing*. Dr. L gave her the code. A sideways glance at Marion showed her head nodding. Good. It was the right one.

"We'll be waiting up front," Marion whispered.

Jem *shifted*. She'd fine-tuned her control over the summer and could now 'flip' it on with very little effort or thought. It actually took more effort to control the dial-a-ghost visual. She *phased* inside, walked past the power room and out into the main lab. The main security panel just inside the front door had a bright red light shining on it. To pass the time, which had lengthened to almost thirty minutes now, she walked around and studied the various pieces of equipment at the team's individual test stations. Some were recognizable, others not. The large control booth along one wall was where Dr. L and Marion could monitor everything.

She was rehearsing her story—which conveniently had large parts of truth—when she felt the first tingle of 'reentry.' She hurried toward the front door. As soon as the *shift* dropped, she carefully entered the code and the light turned green. Grinning, she unlocked and flung the door open with a *"Waa-lah"* flourish.

***

Jem sat quietly at one end of the conference table. Marion had texted all the team members for an emergency meeting and they were waiting for Christine to get here. The way Grathen was watching her, she had a suspicion he already knew what it was about. Jem darted a quick glance sideways. In fact, she was suspicious about a number of things concerning him.

Marion and Dr. L entered, a scowling Christine behind them.

"What is so damn important it couldn't wait until tomorrow?" she snapped. "I was on a date."

"That buffed Adonis that works at ACE Hardware?" Angie asked, grinning.

"Yes. Hopefully, he'll still be available after this better-be-short meeting. I was hoping to inventory his toolbox later tonight."

"*Ooooo,*" Angie crooned.

"Well, we're not the ones drawing it out," Marion said. "Are you two done gossiping?" There were a couple of snickers. "Good. Christine, you need to know the lab security was locked up earlier this evening when the incorrect code was entered on the exterior access panel."

"That's it?" Christine said in disbelief. "Just reset it."

"Tried and failed," Ruben said grimly. Christine's mouth dropped open. "If we can't find and correct the glitch, we'll have to scrub the lab's entire system."

Christine winced. "Has all the lab data been backed up here to the house?"

"No," Marion said, "and we'll be addressing that first thing in the morning. The lab's security has been reset and is now working correctly."

"How?" "What did you do?" Ruben and Christine said on top of each other.

Dr. L exchanged a look with Marion then said, "Jem bypassed it and got us in."

Several stunned seconds later, Ruben exploded. "Impossible! It's a level six system."

"Yes, it took a little bit," Jem replied.

"At least fifteen minutes," Neal said. Everyone looked to him. "I happened to glance out my bedroom window and spotted the doctors at the lab's front door. Couldn't help watching when I realized they were just standing there. Then, imagine my surprise," he said, heavy on the sarcasm, "when Jem opened the lab door."

"She went through the back door," Marion told them with a straight face, "to maintain secrecy."

All eyes dropped to the hand comp laying in front of Jem. It was a decoy, retrieved from her room to keep the subterfuge going.

"Where the hell did you learn how to circumvent a level-six system?" Ruben demanded sharply.

"What about L-7? Can you bypass it?" Christine asked.

"Haven't tried seven—hadn't tried six either, in all honesty, so probably. Where?" Jem shrugged. "No where particular. I noticed a…flaw that appears inherent in most systems." Not being able to detect interdimensional entry could be called a flaw.

"Really?" Half her listeners' eyes lost focus as their genius minds went to work.

"Is that why you keep moving around? New areas, new targets. You must have a pretty big bank account, being the perfect thief and all," Grathen said, sneering.

Back stiff, voice filled with simmering anger, Jem said, "I am not a thief!"

"What? You just browse through wherever? You've obviously practiced."

"It's an intellectual challenge." *You sneering, contemptuous asshole.* "Nothing more. I have never used it wrongly and have no intention to ever do so."

"Nor do we want to have others abuse it *or* Jem," Marion said, "hence the reason for this meeting. We have agreed to keep knowledge of what Jem can do secret and within the Myerstone Research Group. It is now part of your contracts—you can check the addendum later."

"You can't modify my contract without my permission," Grathen said hotly.

"Yes, they can, if it directly pertains to or affects the laboratory's operation," Jonnie said. "It's in the fine print. Although, this instance might be stretching it a bit."

"Not at all," Dr. L said. "Lab operation would have definitely been impacted and critical data lost if we'd had to wipe the system."

"There will be no discussion of this in front of Ned and Janet. In fact, as far as they and anyone else knows, nothing unusual happened tonight. Understood?" Marion's gaze, roaming around the table, stopped on Neal Grathen.

Scowling, he gave a chin jerk of acknowledgement.

Her eyes narrowed for a moment, but then her attention moved on.

"If that's it, I have a date to finish." Christine stood, pointed a finger at Jem. "You and I will talk tomorrow."

"Depends on the subject," Jem returned calmly.

Christine shot her a frown, then turned on her heel. Neal pushed back his chair and followed her out.

"Wow," Angie said, worried lines marring her expression. "Invisibility *and* cyber-genius. If this gets out…there'll be a double bullseye on your back from the entire government and criminal spectrum."

"Jem," Ruben started.

She held up a hand, palm out. "No. I am not discussing it. At all. I'm well aware how this can be misused—see Angie's last comment. If it wasn't for what happened, you'd never have known. And while I trust you," *most of you,* "the more people who know, the more likely the chance of it sneaking out." Picking up her comp, she stood. "Good night, all. See you in the morning."

***

Thunder rumbled in the distance, the next round in the storm system that had kept them indoors for the past two days. August was getting off to a wet start. The rest of the month would probably be a dry scorcher, Jem figured, reaching for another potato. One of the many she and Janet were peeling for the evening meal.

"Jem, are you having problems?"

"No, why?" she asked, brow scrunched in surprise.

"Me and Ned both have seen you getting odd looks from some of them."

"Odd?"

"A kind of frowny puzzled-frustrated look." Janet's scraper paused and she looked up. "A conversation stopped when I walked into a room earlier today. I wouldn't have thought much of it—they are secretive about their work, except I heard your name before I turned the corner. If it's not too personal, can you tell me what's happened? Are you in some kind of trouble?"

Jem worked silently until the potato was done. She both liked and respected the two staff workers and an obvious lie would offend them. Adding the potato to the pot of water with the others, she met Janet's eyes and told a half-lie.

"No, I'm not in trouble. About a week ago, they were trying to figure out how to test another one of their theories. I made what to me was an obvious suggestion. They were, uh, flummoxed?"

Janet threw back her head and laughed heartily. "Oh, Ned will love that. Nothing beats plain ol' common sense. I have a lot of respect for their brains, but sometimes," she grabbed a potato, "it's that forest-tree saying. It's as if they can't process anything simple."

"Granny had a similar saying, that a person could be so smart they're dumb." These two certainly weren't. She'd have to warn the others to be a tad bit more discreet.

There was a bright flash, followed by deep, rolling thunder that rattled the kitchen windows.

Pointing her potato at Jem and her tone turning serious, Janet said, "Watch out for Neal Grathen—his eyes follow you. He's got an ego problem and won't like being shown up. Especially by one of us *inferior* types. He actually called Ned that," she said, outraged.

Beats being called a freak, Jem grumbled silently, reaching for the last tuber. Hearing Angie and Christine's hot responses to Grathen's sarcastic jab had not lessoned the sting. Nor her own deep-down fear that she was. Her scraper slid across the potato, peeling the skin away. Why had she lived, when the others died? Two more slices fell into the bucket between her feet. Why had she been changed? Not just changed, mutated. DNA mutated.

A flurry of strokes finished skinning the potato and she dropped it into the water. Janet carried the pot over to the sink as Jem collected their buckets and went to dump them in the garbage bins behind the garage. Leaning against the doorframe, she absently studied the drenched tree line and pondered Neal Grathen.

He was a growing problem and not just for her. She'd observed a number of clashes between him and the others, not counting the one for name-calling. He'd managed, barely, to stay civil with the doctors two days ago. They were getting tired of it, too, if she was any judge. Jem had a feeling it was only the worry about him going to LE in retribution that kept him from being fired. Janet was right about his attitude. He'd want payback.

It took exactly three weeks and four days to learn just had badly Grathen would betray them all.

Chapter 7

It was late evening, and everyone was relaxing in the den. Or trying to, in the underlying tension permeating the room. Reginald Kurzvall was on Earth and had sent word he'd be at Myerstone tomorrow. No one expected it to be a pleasant visit. The doctors were talking, reviewing data in the conference room.

Jem had been watching Jonnie teach a new card game to Ruben, Angie, and Christine for the past hour. Neal, as usual, mostly ignored them all and was reading something on his hand comp. Yawning, she decided to head up to her room. She and Ned had worked pretty hard today.

She'd reached the top of the stairs when Grathen brushed past her without a word of warning or apology. *Jerk.* Her eyes narrowed as he turned into his room. That was an awful hurried step for someone just planning on watching a movie or showering or something. She heard the lock engage as she passed his door. She stopped, turned and eyed it.

Wariness turned into worry. He was up to something and she doubted it was good. She bit her lip, then, decision made, she cast a wary glance around. *Shifted. Phased* through his bedroom door.

"…no, nothing's changed," she heard Grathen say.

He was sitting in front of his table comp, which was in comm mode. A middle-aged, non-descript man on its screen was frowning out at him. "We did a low-power energy run yesterday—got some interesting readings."

"But they're still refusing to run a full-powered transfer test?"

"Yes, sir."

Shit, damn, crap. He was telling this guy about the project. Not for the first time either, she fumed, listening to some of the questions the man was asking. The doctors were going to blow a gasket when she told them. No way they'd keep him on the team now. Wondering just how much Grathen had revealed, she got her answer.

"This Jem Wilmont is as interesting as the cannon. She's still there? Good. I've had her investigated. She's a nobody drifter with no family. They couldn't have found a more perfect test subject. I intend to speak with her after I arrive in the morning."

"My fee?"

"I'll have a cash card with me." The screen blanked.

Kurzvall. It had to be him. Jem's fury boiled over and she saw red. Literally, as something inside wrenched and the monochrome of nothingness sheared away.

"You sorry son of a bitch!"

He jerked around.

"You told Kurzvall about *me*." Her fists balled. She'd have punched him except he jumped out of his chair and backed away from her. Turning instead to his door, she yanked on it. Giving vent to a frustrated growl, she snapped the lock open. Flinging the door wide, she stepped out into the hall and began yelling for Marion and Dr. L.

Being closer, the team members got there first. The doctors rushed up behind them.

"What? What's going on?" Marion demanded over Angie's shoulder.

Jem's arm swung out and pointed into the bedroom. "This…this *asshole* sold information about the project. About *me* to Kurzvall."

There were a couple of creative curses and the room filled with bodies and hostility. Dr. L pushed his way to the front. "Is this true? Have you violated your contract? The non-disclosure agreement?"

"Me?" Grathen snapped, his body language belligerent. "Kurzvall is funding us—all of this." He waved an arm. "He's entitled to know what we're doing, what we've accomplished. You're the ones breaching contract since he's not received a report for six months. I've merely given him an unofficial one."

"Then you wouldn't have needed to be paid for it," Christine snapped.

"What, *exactly*, have you told him?" Marion demanded, her voice a mixture of anger and disgust.

His chin came up. "That we'd successfully done a transference."

"With fatalities," Ruben said through clenched teeth.

"Yes, but Jem survived." He shot Jem a veiled look. "I haven't told him everything about her."

Jem figured everyone heard the unspoken *yet*. "He also said something about a cannon. Don't know what—" She stopped when everyone went pale, cussed, or did both.

"No wonder he's been demanding we restart testing," Dr. L said tiredly, running a hand across his face. "I can't believe—we all agreed to keep that private. Undisclosed and not in any report."

Uh-oh. Whatever it was, it was bad. Grathen had betrayed the whole team, professionally and personally. "What is it?" Jem asked, even as she dreaded the answer.

Face drawn, Dr. L turned to her. "That's why we were trying to get back into the lab the night it locked up. We wanted to check the data on a couple of tests we'd run earlier."

"Which was still on just the lab's server," Jem said, remembering.

"Yes. Jonnie came to us that evening with a theory that was… disturbing. It's still theoretical, mind you, but the initial data analysis supports it."

"Supports what, Doc?"

"Whether or not we can work out the original transference goal, the Otanak field could also be used in another, intentionally destructive manner."

"In short," Christine said grimly, "a cannon to blow up Otanak engines."

"A cannon of unstoppable devastation," Jonnie said in a stone-hard voice, "since the field would be interdimensional until it came in contact with another engine."

"Then *boom*. Like the mail pod," Angie added.

"Do you know what the military would give for such a weapon?" Marion said.

The same dread in her voice swept through Jem. "Kurzvall undoubtedly does."

"Neal Grathen, you're dismissed, effective immediately. Ruben, lock him out of our system," Marion said brusquely.

"With pleasure," the man replied darkly before leaving.

Grathen's glare was downright venomous.

"Pack your stuff," Marion continued. "I want you gone by noon tomorrow. Don't bother listing any of us as referrals as it certainly won't get you hired."

"He already has another employer," Jonnie snarked. "Kurzvall bought more than information."

"You'll regret this, all of you," Grathen said, malice in both voice and eyes.

"The only thing I regret is that this project will be turned on its head," Dr. L said. "We intended it to improve and simplify lives, not come up with another means to end them."

"May not come to that, at least not yet," Angie said, glaring at Grathen. "Kurzvall isn't going to want the real information of what we're doing to get out either. Others will jump on the idea and the first to win that race will be very rich."

The Myerstone's website simply listed the group as researching the various aspects of Otanak fields and their effectiveness in starship engines.

"We'll have to just wait and see what happens tomorrow," Marion said. Dr. L nodded. "Noon," she snapped at Grathen before turning and walking out.

The others gave him various dirty looks before leaving, too. Jem was the last one remaining.

"You invaded my privacy," he accused her.

Jem snorted. "So? After what you've done to mine, and to your supposed teammates, you should be damn glad I don't kick you in the balls."

His eyes suddenly narrowed. "How did you get in? The door was locked."

Oops. "The perfect thief—remember?—leaves no trace of their passage." Hopefully, he wouldn't wonder why she would have locked up behind her.

"Uh-huh." His voice turned sly. "Kurzvall—probably a lot of people—would be interested in that."

Jem's lip curled. "A threat?" She sauntered to his doorway, turned. Holding his gaze with her own, she lightly tapped the door with her knuckles. It was a reminder, a warning, and a threat all rolled into one. "Best think about that. Everybody has to sleep sometime."

Grathen's face went dark with anger.

In her room, Jem pulled a soda from the mini-fridge, still fuming. The snot had a lot of nerve complaining about privacy. She wasn't the one sneaking around and betraying… Her thoughts trailed off as a sudden realization hit her. It couldn't have been more than ten minutes between her *shift* in the hallway and her confronting Grathen.

Staring blankly at the wall, Jem mentally replayed the scene in his room. There, that wrench, when she was so furious. Hope swelled. Could she do it again? *No time like now*. Taking a deep breath, she *shifted*.

She spent several minutes kinda-sorta feeling around in her brain. Kinda-sorta found something she couldn't put a name to. Wishing herself luck, she mentally yanked on it, hard…and found herself holding a sweating, cold bottle. Another deep breath.

Shift. Monochrome grayness, no sensations.

Yank. Bright color and a cold bottle.

Her grin was so wide it hurt.

***

Kurzvall arrived mid-morning. Jem and Ned paused in pulling the tarp off the mower as the dark gray limo pulled up to the front of the house. The driver jumped out and went around to open the back door. Even from a distance, Jem could see the arrogance on the passenger as he stepped out and walked toward the house.

"Wonder how long it'll take for the fireworks to start," she mused.

"Fireworks?"

Jem tugged on the tarp, letting the heavy cover fall to the ground. "Yeah. He's been pushing for them to run full power tests. They say they're not ready—need more information. Which is why they've been doing those small runs and late-night research."

"And he thinks he can tell them that, why?"

"He's the foundation's main funding source."

"Maybe he likes paying for equipment and walls," Ned said dryly.

Jem snickered as he popped the mower's top, pulling the oil stick out to check it. Must have been okay, as he re-inserted it and closed the lid. She climbed onto the seat. Battery? Charged. She pressed the starter and the engine engaged. Four-plus acres should keep her away from the brewing storm.

She worked until mid-afternoon, finally parking the mower in its spot.

She was tired, dusty, and hungry. She'd skipped lunch, after seeing Kurzvall behind the lab and waving his arm at her. She'd pretended it was a 'hello' wave, waved back, then ignored the subsequent arm movements and kept on mowing. On the far side of the acreage.

The limo was gone now, as was Grathen's car. She gave a mental *yay* as she dismounted. Unwinding the charger cord behind the rider's seat, she was plugging it into the power outlet when Ned came around the corner.

"Done?" he asked.

"Need to do the area around and in front of the house. Figured I'd do that after getting a sandwich or something. Didn't want to stop earlier."

"Uh-huh." He chuckled. "Come on in. Janet's got sandwiches ready for us." At Jem's surprised look, he added, "Kind of kept myself busy outside, too."

"Was it that big a blow-up?"

"Don't rightly know. They were in the house for about an hour or so. Then they went out to the lab and stayed there until Kurzvall left. Don't like him. Or that driver of his that was nosin' around. Bet he doubles as a bodyguard. Had to run him out of the maintenance shed," Ned said, scowling.

They paused outside the back door and Jem used her hat to smack as much dust off herself as possible. Ned brushed grassy bits off her back and shoulders. Jem gave a relieved sigh as she sat down at the kitchen table, both at the food Janet was placing in front of them and the interior coolness.

Janet poured herself a glass of water and sat next to Ned. "Dr. L is in a grumpy mood; Marion's is down-right foul," she announced without fanfare.

Jem nearly choked. A couple of coughs managed to get the bite down the right passage. Foul? She hadn't thought Marion even capable of it.

"The others are skulking around—moods range from irritated to pissed. I done told them we're leaving early, Ned. I'm not putting up with a house full of snarly attitudes. Neal Grathen was bad enough, but at least he's gone now."

Ned's eyebrows came back down from his hairline. "This fella really set them off?"

"Uh-huh. They came out of the conference room with their jaws set and fire in Christine's eyes. Whatever they got into in the lab only made it worse. Jem, there's plenty of sandwich fixings, chips, and a jar of those spicy pickles Ruben's mother sends. Y'all can manage supper."

"Yes, ma'am."

"Guess I'll finish up the hedge pruning tomorrow," Ned said, taking a bite. Chewed, swallowed, looked over at Jem. "Consider your day done, too, after the yard's finished."

The rest of their late lunch was eaten in silence. Jem went out to finish mowing while Ned put away tools he'd been using. She was out front, next to the driveway, when their truck passed her. She returned their waves. Throttling down to idle, Jem watched the battered truck dwindle down the long driveway, then turn left on the main road.

She turned her gaze to the house.

Jem no longer blamed the ones inside for what had happened. Or how she'd changed. Might as well blame the Universe's proverbial wheel-of-fate. Yes, they'd sidestepped a few legalities, but they'd been forced to make tough decisions under terrible circumstances. They'd shielded her, keeping her safe. They'd become friends as they helped her through the chaos, always treating her as a person and never as a lab rat. Which is certainly how Kurzvall viewed her.

Yep, this Reginald Kurzvall was going to be a pain in the butt. An even worse one once Grathen spilled everything about her—no reason not to now. Probably for another fee; maybe a job somewhere in Kurzvall's

organization. Or just plain spite.

Jem sighed, put the mower blades in gear. It was time to move on.

Chapter 8

Angie was dealing the next round of cards when Ruben came in from the front of the house.

"Guess whose limo is pulling up in front?" he said sourly.

There were two *shits* and one f-bomb.

"I didn't hear anything about him coming back tonight," Angie grumbled.

"Don't think he told anyone," Jonnie said. "Dr L has been logged into the Geneva Science Base Library for the past couple of hours doing some intense research." He looked around. "Anyone know where Marion got to?"

"She went into town," Jem told him. "Said she needed to get away for a while." Christine had left too, planning on visiting her boyfriend when he got off work.

The doorbell rang. No one moved. A second ring.

"You know," Jem drawled, laying her cards down, "we don't have to let him in."

There was an impatient double ring as Jem reached the front door. Pulling it open, she stepped out, forcing Kurzvall to take a step back, and closed it behind her. "The doctors are not receiving visitors this evening," she said politely, using a phrase she'd heard in her travels.

"I'm here to see you, Miss Wilmont."

The sun was still high enough for her to see the flash of avarice across his face. Yep, Grathen tattled. Jem braced herself. "Why?"

"I want to hire you."

"Why?" she repeated.

"A recent conversation with Neal Grathen proved to be very enlightening. I can use someone with your skills in my organization."

Uh-huh. "I don't do corporate espionage."

A haughty eyebrow winged up. "No, but you could stop it. Investigate suspicious circumstances. Provide support in other areas as needed," he said smoothly.

Too smooth and too vague. His gaze went over her shoulder.

Half-turned, she found the others packed in a window. Jem couldn't help grinning at how Jonnie's nose was squished against the glass.

"Thank you, but no," she said, turning back.

"I offer an excellent salary and benefits—a lot more than you're getting here," he added, contempt sneaking into his voice.

Something about him set her teeth on edge. "Not interested. To be truthful, Mr. Kurzvall, I don't like you," she informed him, still polite.

"Not a requirement; only that you do what you're told," he said, his words edged with annoyance.

She studied the driver-bodyguard leaning against the car for a moment. He was watching her very intently. *Does he know too?* Before she could respond, the door opened behind her and Dr. L stepped out. Irritation fairly oozed off him.

"I told you I'd send a report in the next couple of days. Why are you here?" Dr. L's finger stopped just short of poking Kurzvall in the chest. "Your incessant demands that we resume testing are unrealistic, unreasonable, and…and…*wrong*. We've told you, repeatedly, it's not safe. We need more information. We need a better understanding about how the Otanak fields function, how they interact with other fields across the spectrum."

"Those small prods you're doing won't tell you much, if anything. You need to duplicate the test run that transported Wilmont here."

"And killed two people," Angie yelled through the window.

"Accidents are often unavoidable when science pushes past known boundaries and well into new terrain." Kurzvall's chin pointed at Jem, probably for emphasis.

Jem let out a loud, derisive snort. "So, 'shit happens' is okay with you? I lost a friend in that 'accident'." It was a doubly good thing Grathen hadn't known the full extent of her mutation.

"If it's the price for that knowledge, yes. Speaking of which, I expect you to resume experimentation, *fully*, by the end of the month. If it's additional equipment or resources you require, funding will be increased to cover it."

How many times could this guy be told NO?

Dr. L's shoulders squared and his expression hardened. The mild-mannered professor Jem knew and liked had morphed into a fiery-eyed warrior. *Oh, wow.*

"That won't be necessary, Mr. Kurzvall," Dr. L said brusquely. "In fact, we will no longer expect or accept *any* funding from Kurzvall Industries. I hereby terminate our association. Immediately."

Shock replaced the haughty look Kurzvall had worn since his arrival.

"We will seek funding elsewhere. Once we announce our true goal, *transference*, I expect we will have more than enough credits to operate."

"You can't do that," Kurzvall sputtered, his face turning a splotchy red.

"The Myerstone Research Group is an independent, private organization. Contrary to your belief, we are not owned by you. We are free to choose where and from whom we receive funds from or associate with."

"You insignificant, odious—"

Dr. L's hand flew up. "Leave. Now. Or I'll have you escorted off my property."

Ruben and Jonnie tumbled out the doorway and flanked the doctor. Their scowls said they'd be more than happy to help Kurzvall comply. Kurzvall's man straightened, took several steps toward them.

Jem watched Kurzvall's fists clench and unclench several times. Oh yeah, Mr. High-and-Mighty was pissed. Bet he was usually the one doing the dumping. His eyes caught Jem's when he turned to leave. A chill snaked down her spine at the promise she read in them.

"Good riddance," Dr. L said, earning a sideways look from Jem.

Jonnie cleared his throat. "Uh, what about Marion?"

"She will be ecstatic. She's been recommending terminating our association with Reginald Kurzvall for several months, but I was hesitant to do so." He grimaced. "Today has proven her right. We should have done this months ago."

The limo's tires spit gravel and dust as it executed a hard, fast about-face.

Dr. L shook his head and went back into the house. The others followed.

Jem watched the limo speed down the driveway. Intuition sat up and waved a flag. "He'll be back," she whispered to the sinking sun.

***

Two days later, her intuition proved right.

Kurzvall returned, demanding a copy of their project data for another lab he planned to start up elsewhere. "I want all of it, not just what you've been dribbling to me in those ridiculously bland reports."

"All data created by the Myerstone Project belongs to the Myerstone Group," Dr. Lammstein told him firmly. "It's stated explicitly so in our contract, which is why your reports were only summaries. You will not be getting one data bit."

Jem hadn't realized a face could literally turn purple. Kurzvall went a lightyear past livid and the conversation really went downhill at that point.

Finally, Marion held up a hand. "You, sir, had better leave before I call the Enforcers and have you arrested for all those threats you are spouting," she said, fury coloring each word. "And I swear on my doctoral thesis, if you ever set foot or tire on our property again, I *will* call them."

"Go ahead, call them now," Kurzvall sneered. "I'm sure they'd love to hear what really happened to the UPMS hanger."

Jem stiffened. Neither doctor batted an eye.

"As project leaders, Marion and I have taken full responsibility for both the destruction and the deaths. We expect to face the consequences, and if it comes sooner than later?" He shrugged. "So be it."

Marion's chin lifted. "We also stand by our subsequent actions…or inactions. While our decisions might not have been legally correct, we believe they were the right ones, given all factors."

"And the rest of us stand with them," Ruben Davis said, stepping into the conference room. The rest of the team filled the doorway behind him, their heads bobbing in agreement.

Kurzvall turned his glare on Jem.

She crossed her arms and repeated Dr. L's shrug. Nothing she could do to stop either him or Grathen from talking about her. But, being stable—thanks to those decisions—she should be able to handle any fallout, including persistent scientists. Her lips lifted in a grin, thinking how easy it'd be to avoid them.

Evidently taking her grin as a personal affront, Kurzvall stormed out, his face a dark mask.

Jem finished packing her belongings that night. Logging in online, she hunted up a decent-looking transit hotel and reserved a room for five days. That should be plenty of time to decide what to do and where to do it.

She said her final good-byes next morning, even getting a gruff "Hate to see you go" from Ned. Jem climbed into Christine's sedan, and neither of them spoke much on the drive to her hotel near the airport. As the car turned into the parking lot, a flight of butterflies launched in her stomach. *This was it.*

Putting the car in park, engine idling, Christine turned to her. "Jem…"

Jem's lips twisted into a smile. "I'll miss you, too. All of you. Can't say I liked the circumstances, but I'm glad I got to know you."

"If you ever need us…if something comes up, don't hesitate to contact me. Us." Her smile wavered. "Oh, screw it. Stay in contact anyway, okay?"

"I will." Jem grinned, waggled her eyebrows. "Even if you don't see me."

Christine gave her a light punch on the shoulder. "Don't you dare."

Jem did something she rarely did, except with Dani. She reached over and gave the woman a hug. Getting out, she pulled her travel bag and backpack from the back seat. With a final wave and a deep breath, she headed into the hotel…and whatever the future held.

Chapter 9

"Jem, come back to the lab. Quick. Something terrible has happened."

Jem frowned down at Marion's text message, wondering for the hundredth time what had happened since leaving yesterday. Other than one *"Hurry, please,"* there'd been no other responses to her texts over the past two hours. There'd been no response of any kind from texts or calls to the other team members…even Dr. L.

The auto-cab halted in front of the house and an interior light came on for human convenience as twilight was long gone. "Please pay amount indicated on panel," the customer-pleasing digital voice announced. Cash card ready, Jem hurriedly inserted it in the payment slot, the doors unlocking several seconds later. "Thank you and have a pleasant day." As soon as Jem exited, the light snapped off and it turned itself around. Its electronic brain would reverse the directions Jem had furnished to return to the city. She'd spend the night in her old room here and catch a ride back tomorrow.

A single light burned in the house's lower level. Jem hurried around the corner. The lab came into view as she passed the garage. Not only was the door's overhead light on, but so was the red experiment-underway caution light next to it. A quick look at the vehicles as she passed through the parking area told her the entire team was here. She paused mid-step. *Wait, that's Neal Grathen's car. What's he doing here?* Temper briefly overcame worry. He and Kurzvall had to be behind whatever had happened. Jem pushed the lab door open and stopped just inside the entrance, scanning the silent room. Blinking lights on the equipment indicated they were all on, as expected, but there was no sign of anyone. Here or through the control booth's wide window.

What the hell was going on? Were they back in the power room?

"Marion? Dr. L?" she called out loudly.

No response. Her stomach clenched as her intuition screamed *bad, bad.*

Jem moved toward the control booth. "*Marion!*" she gasped, close enough now to see the woman draped over a counter. Flinging open the door, she nearly screamed at the sight of bodies crumpled on the floor. Rushing in, she felt for Marion's pulse; it was beating. She quickly checked the others: all alive. What the frigging hell had happened?

Later. Medics now.

Whipping around, her first sight was the childish look of glee on Grathen's face as he filled the booth's doorway. The next was of the funny looking weapon in his hand. *A dart gun?*

"You'll make me doubly rich."

A sharp jab in her shoulder was followed by an explosion of pain throughout her entire body. There wasn't even time to scream before unconsciousness engulfed her.

***

Jem woke propped up next to the booth door and to pain. A burning, throbbing pain everywhere. She couldn't hold back a moan.

"You're awake?"

"Hurts. Can't move," she said through gritted teeth.

"The fire part is usually gone by the time a person wakes for the paralysis part, which you shouldn't be yet. I knew that screwy system of yours would be a problem," came Grathen's low mutter. Louder, he added, "The others got a second, longer-lasting drug since I didn't know how long it'd take you to get here."

"It was you…Marion's phone," she managed between the sheets of fire cascading down her legs. "Why?"

"Needed to lure you back, of course. For the making me rich part," he snickered.

Jem silently cursed both him and Kurzvall. Through pain-filled, watery eyes, she could see Grathen busy doing something on the main console. Doing what was answered when a deep hum filled the room. He'd activated the power generator, and it was running at full strength.

"What are…you doing?"

"Getting what's due to me," came his sneering reply. "Ruben Davis thought he was so smart. Yet he never found my backdoor, a hidden account I had installed. An *admin* account. Had to activate it from here, though." He scowled down at Marion. "Didn't expect to be locked out of the main system without notice."

He'd downloaded their project data. With administrator permissions, he'd have access to everything in both the main house and the lab systems. "They'll report—"

"No one will be reporting anything," he interrupted savagely, as the generator's steady hum changed to a throbbing beat. "I've disabled the safety governor. Once the power couplings short, nothing will stop it."

Horrified, Jem whispered "*No*" as he moved to stand over her. "Please, don't do this." All she got was a demonic grin, followed by a bolt of pain that flung her into unconsciousness when he grabbed her.

***

She found herself slung over Grathen's shoulder when consciousness returned, his footsteps crunching as he moved. *Gravel,* whispered Jem's dazed brain. Pain still burned all through her. She couldn't stop the half-scream when Grathen's sudden stop jarred her. The grip on her legs tightened.

"What the hell?" an unknown voice demanded.

Enforcers? Jem's brief hope they'd somehow been alerted died at Grathen's response.

"Why are you…meet after…Kurzvall's place."

Kurzvall, like she'd thought. Jem struggled to hear over the pain and the throbbing in her ears, over the darkness threatening to take her again.

"Boss didn't…ou get it?"

"…my backpack…"

A high-pitched whine punched through the pain. *The generator.*

Arguing…yelling…sounds that no longer made sense to her sluggish brain.

Rough hands pulled her off Grathen's shoulder and it all disappeared into a black whirlpool.

***

She woke, still paralyzed, with pain radiating down her spine and all four limbs. Jem gritted her teeth to keep from crying out, but a tear leaked from one eye as she forced them open. A bedroom? Felt like a bed under her.

"Good, you're awake."

Kurzvall. The bastard. Standing over her. Frowning?

"You appear to still be in pain. Dougson, didn't you say the drug's first stage was short term?"

"That's what the specs said."

The voice answering was the same one she'd heard outside the lab. Jem recognized him when he moved to stand beside his boss. It was the driver-bodyguard.

"A half-hour or so," Dougson continued. "Long enough for the paralysis to take effect."

"Hmmm. Must be her system. Grethen did say it'd been affected by the O-field transport. No matter. Welcome, Miss Wilmont. I'm sure you've gathered by now where you are. To be blunt, you now work for me. You will follow my orders, and of those I place over you." Dougson leered. "You will have no opinion or say in said orders. You will have no communication or contact with others than what I allow. If you try running, or causing me any form of trouble or embarrassment, there will be consequences. How, you ask, will I enforce that?" His smile wasn't pleasant. "I'll let Dougson explain. Five minutes," he told Dougson, then turned and left the room.

"Remember that tracker the Myerstone people had you wear?"

Dougson moved down toward her feet. Cascades of agony nearly sent back into unconsciousness when he lifted her leg, bringing the tracker into view. "Well, we appropriated it from Grathen, along with his dart gun. Amazing what the guy had lifted. Pretty sure he had plans of his own concerning you." He moved back up.

"The boss has the remote controller. You do something that we don't like…" Dougson held up a hand and mimicked pressing a button. "However, you should know we replaced their gentle sedative with what Grathen had in his darts. It's called Fire and Ice. Never heard of the drug before, but it certainly makes an effective penalty for misbehaving employees. Then, of course, there'll be punishment," he said, stepping closer.

Jem closed her eyes as he ran his hands over her. Cupped her breasts and ran his thumbs over her nipples. "I can think of all sorts of… punishments." Teeth gritted, she endured his pawing from her crotch to her cheeks.

"Dougson," Kurzvall called out.

"By the way," he ran a finger down her face, "we'll also kill anyone you involve or enlist to help." Leaning down, he whispered, "Misbehave."

She lay there, humiliation coursing more hotly through her than the drug and silently swearing like those workers on the fishing trawler.

"How much longer before the drug wears off?" she heard Kurzvall ask.

"Specs say another two hours or so," Dougson answered. "Depends on when Grathen dosed her and that system of hers. Since the first part is running longer, the paralysis might too."

"Arrangements need to be made for transferring her to my ship, preferably without any—" He paused at the sound of a knock on a door. The door to her room was swiftly shut and locked.

She heard murmuring voices, then nothing. Total silence. They must have left. Jem strained. If she could…just…move…*some*thing. She had to get away. No way was she spending years doing all sorts of dirty work. Or pleasing Dougson and whoever else. She shuddered. *Wait. I shuddered.* Minuscule as it was, it was movement. *Yes!*

The throbbing pain down her spine wasn't as bad now, either. Her fingers and toes? Just a tingle. And…her left big toe wiggled. *Halleluiah!* It was wearing off. Two hours? She'd see about that. Time passed as she strained and wiggled and strained some more.

A door slammed in the outer room. Jem froze. *Click*, the lock disengaged and the bedroom door opened. Dougson stuck his head in. Leered.

Jem held her breath. Would he notice one leg wasn't positioned as it had been?

"How's the pain?"

"Manageable," she lied, projecting a sullen tone. All she had was an occasional throb in her neck.

He grinned. "Don't go anywhere," he said, then closed the door.

"Funny," Jem muttered. She resumed stretching and flexing her muscles.

***

Standing on wobbly legs, Jem *shifted*. She *phased* through the door, finding herself in the open living area of a large suite. A compact kitchen was to her left and a computer niche was tucked in the corner on her right. The hallway undoubtedly led to bedrooms and such. With no sight or sound of either bastard, she stopped the *shift*. All that practicing was paying off now.

She'd about made herself dizzy, popping in and out of it like some kid's game, all the while ignoring any thoughts about bodily effects. Her 'time' had also expanded again, to about thirty-five minutes. Unless there was a significant break between the shifts to reset her internal timer, it was cumulative. One more frigging thing that didn't make sense. Although having to rebuild energy afterwards before being able to *shift* again did.

Jem began searching for the remote controller. She couldn't leave without it. Naturally, the SOB wasn't thoughtful enough to leave it laying out, like Grathen's gun left on a counter. Darts were piled beside it. The ones they'd undoubtedly drained for her tracker. Nothing she could do about that at the moment. She spotted a backpack in a corner chair. Zipping it open, she wrinkled her nose at the wadded up hideous shirt on top. Yep, Grathen's. Rummaging, she found two cash cards, a hand computer, and various personal items, but no controller.

A quick scan of the comp showed it not only held Myerstone's data and research files, but the frigging asshole had copied the team's personal files as well. Jaw set, she started to delete everything but stopped, finger poised. Erasing it would be the same as erasing them. What they'd worked so hard for. *Died* for. Grief and a different pain engulfed her and she swayed. *No, not now. Grieve later.* Reluctantly, she dropped it back into the bag. She'd find some way to keep—

"Have the pilot put the ship on standby."

Jem froze as Kurzvall's voice came through the door. Dropped the backpack in the chair. *Shifted.*

"I can't leave," Kurzvall said caustically as he entered, "now that I've been *informed* of the lab explosion. I'll be expected to express my condolences at the team's loss, give some kind of statement, and—damn reporters," he swore. "Nothing but leeches."

She glared at Kurzvall, fury and disgust roiling in her guts. Her friends had meant nothing to him. Switched her rage to Dougson when he trailed in behind him. Bastards. She'd have to play their game for now, which meant going back in that damn bedroom and pretending to just be getting mobile. *My turn will come*, she vowed to herself, starting to cross the room.

"Has our guy in security wiped the video feed for this floor? Good. I want a round-the-clock guard outside the door."

"Hotel management won't like it."

"Don't care. Wilmont might risk running, gambling on getting the band off before we find she's gone. Making this useless."

Jem whipped around, her eyes widening as he pulled the remote out of a jacket pocket. *Bingo!*

"She can't work her magic without her hand comp," Dougson said. "The one in the backpack was Grathen's with the lab data. We'll need to retrieve hers from wherever she was staying."

Huh. Kurzvall hadn't told him about her invisibility.

"How's our newest employee?"

"Still frozen when I checked on her, though she said the pain was 'manageable.' Means the drug should be wearing off soon. Don't know how Grathen managed to get what's supposed to be a new drug for law enforcement use only."

Kurzvall gave him a cool stare.

"I won't have trouble acquiring it, either," Dougson hastily added.

"Obtain a supply before we leave for Hebros. We'll need to run a few tests to determine exactly how long each state lasts on her specific system."

Bastards!

"You can take the first watch on the door. Dismissed."

"Yes, sir."

This is my chance, Jem thought as Dougson walked out. Kurzvall glanced toward the bedroom, a satisfied smile on his face. Maneuvering around behind him, Jem *shifted* back and, with a satisfied smile of her own, gave him a well-deserved kick in the ass. He slammed into a small side table, the remote flying off to land not far from the backpack. Jem grabbed up both, tossing one into the other as Kurzvall yelled for Dougson. She showed him her finger and *shifted*.

"What the hell?"

The look of utter shock on Kurzvall's face stopped Jem in mid-step.

"Did she just *vanish*?" Dougson sputtered from the open doorway.

"Shut the damn door," Kurzvall yelled, then erupted in a string of curses as he pushed himself up.

He hadn't known! Jem stared, shocked. Appalled. Grathen hadn't told them. *And I've just provided a demo. Shit, damn, crap.*

Dougson slammed the door. "I didn't feel anything. Maybe she's still here?"

"Would you be? Grathen. That sonofabitch." Kurzvall's fists clenched. "Son. Of. A. *Bitch*! That's why he snickered when he spoke about her being *invisible* to electronics."

"I'd say her system was damn well 'affected' alright," Dougson snarked.

"If he wasn't already dead, I'd kill him myself," Kurzvall swore. "He was planning on utilizing that ability himself. That's why he had the tracker and dart gun in the—*the backpack!* The bitch took it and the hand comp."

Satisfaction swept through her as Kurzvall swore some more. He'd never get his greedy hands on their data if she had anything to do with it.

Kurzvall pointed a finger at Dougson. "Not a word. To anybody.

About invisibility or data. Understood?"

"Yes, sir."

"Don't move from that door. Be ready, in case we got lucky. Grathen's thirty-minute comment makes sense now. He had to be referring to her invisibility, not the electronic override as the asshole led me to believe."

Dougson gave his boss a nonplussed look. "How do I stop something I can't see?"

Kurzvall sneered. "Figure it out. I need to think."

Jem shook her head and *phased* through the wall, leaving Kurzvall poring a drink and Dougson scanning the room nervously. She'd *shift* back as soon as she could find a safe spot.

Chapter 10

Jem huddled in a chair, staring in horrified numbness at the wall viewscreen, barely hearing the newscaster's solemn droning in the background. Bright lights lit the scene as firemen and other responders searched in the pre-dawn darkness through the charred remains of the main house. The team's vehicles were burned, upended wrecks. No sign of the lab building itself, only a concrete slab and twisted, unidentifiable chunks strewn everywhere.

One of the responders waved a hand, and the camera followed a man in white coveralls as he ran over with a black bag. A small, black bag. Jem swallowed, knowing what they were carefully placing in it, adding it to the others on a nearby gurney. Unable to take anymore, she cut the screen off. She closed her eyes—a mistake. The image of their sprawled bodies flashed before her. An image forever imprinted in her memory.

Stumbling over to her travel bag, she pulled out the bottle of expensive whisky the team had given her as a going away gift. Her hindbrain said that was a stupid idea. She rudely told it what she thought. Her room was locked tight, Kurzvall wouldn't try anything yet—even if he knew where she was, and she needed oblivion.

***

Jem parked on the side of the road. Guards were preventing any non-authorized personnel from going onto the property. That was okay with her. Not so much for the two reporters she could hear grumbling beside the van a couple of car lengths away. Standing next to her rental, Jem stared at the activity she could see across the field. The field she had mowed only days ago. She ignored the vehicle pulling in behind hers, figuring it to be another looky-loo.

There was a crunch of steps on gravel. Then, "Jem?"

She turned. It was Ned, his features heavy with grief.

"Ned. I saw the news…I had to see for myself." She brushed away tears she hadn't felt until then.

He nodded slowly, his gaze going to the distant activity.

They stood silent. Just watching. The reporters scrambled forward as an ambulance came down the driveway. One stood practically in the road, camera held up and probably already recording. The other one shouted questions at the driver as he paused before pulling onto the road toward town.

"Leeches," Jem muttered, her eyes following it. Knowing what it carried.

"Aye," Ned said, glaring at them.

She turned. Hesitated. "How are you and Janet doing?"

"We're doin' okay, mostly. But it's hard, especially for my wife. She interacted with them more than me, workin' outside like I did. We were hired right after they bought the place several years back." Silence. "Lucky you left when you did."

"Sometimes," she said softly, her gaze on the charred roof, "surviving is the hardest." She caught his swift look in her peripheral vision. Maybe that had revealed more than she'd like. Maybe that would have him wondering about her. Maybe she'd give a shit later.

"I was headed into town, but that can wait. It's nearly supper time and we'd both be pleased to have you join us." He jerked his thumb over his shoulder. "Our place is just down the road."

Jem's stomach roiled at the mention of food. She was still recovering, not to mention that quality time with the toilet bowl not too many hours ago. At least the headache was gone. She thought of the band still around her ankle that needed taking care of. The remote's pieces had been deposited in several recycling units. Nor would Kurzvall let her slip away. But those were future issues. Here and now, she was mighty short on friends.

She gave Ned a wry smile. "I'm not up to eating much, but I'd be pleased to join you."

As it turned out, none of them ate much. They were sitting around, sharing memories when Law Enforcement Detectives Alfred LeBlanc and Cella White came to the door. They'd gotten Ned and Janet's name and address from Myerstone's banking records. They'd gotten hers, too, and were more than happy to cross her interview off their to-do list. They asked the standard investigative questions, then focused on Myerstone's activities.

"There was another explosion, back in December of last year," said Detective White. The young detective looked at her notes. "What can you tell us about that?"

Jem let Ned and Janet answer most of those questions. She'd explained about being hired as seasonal help and released just a few days ago.

"Guess it's a good thing you left when you did," Detective LeBlanc said, eyeing her thoughtfully. "Any problems with them?"

"No, sir. In fact, I got to be friends with several of them."

"Where are you working now?"

"Nowhere yet."

They noted the transit hotel she was staying at, then politely asked her not to leave the area until their investigation was completed. LeBlanc also asked to update them if she found a more permanent place.

Jem left shortly after the Enforcers did, Ned and Janet eliciting a promise from her to stay in touch. A promise she didn't know if she could keep, as it could put them in danger.

"We'll also kill anyone you involve or enlist to help."

Jem had to pull over for a short time, waiting for the shudders to stop as her time in Kurzvall and Dougson's hands hit hard. Reaching her hotel, she removed the backpack from the trunk. She hadn't searched it yet. Time now for dumpster diving, in a manner of speaking. Her nose crinkled. Those shirts were definitely trash.

Chapter 11

Not knowing how long it'd take the Enforcers to close their investigation, Jem had rented a small apartment on the second floor of her landlord's home. Mr. Caleb Petrov was an elderly widower. His only child was in military service off-planet and Jem figured he was lonely. He was usually sitting on the porch or in the front room, weather depending, when she arrived from work, so she'd stop and chat with the garrulous old-timer for a few minutes before climbing the stairs. Jem had a sneaky feeling she'd become a kid-substitute.

She'd also taken a retail job in a flower shop. Jem was on her lunch break in the back room of *The Exquisite Bouquet* when Cassie Madden waddled in and collected her lunch from the employee refrigeration. Waddled being the correct description, as she was very heavily pregnant. Swallowing, Jem asked if she was sure there were only two in there. Cassie's answering smile was a bright white against her dark skin.

"Yep. I have them check at every appointment." She lowered into a chair opposite Jem. "Don't know where the extra one came from as there's none in either mine or Jose's families."

"Maybe the Universe decided to be kind."

"Well, the Universe can come help change diapers."

Jem laughed.

"You know, I think that's the first laugh I've heard from you in the three weeks you've been here."

Jem blinked. "Really?"

"Really. You smile, but there's shadows in your eyes. Jadine put up the closed sign and left to go have lunch with her husband," she said, forking up a bite of her salad. "Just you and me here, if you'd like to talk while the boss is away."

Jem blinked again, then took a bite while she considered it. A quick glance through her eyelashes showed Cassie calmly eating, waiting without pushing. She'd cracked open the door; it was up to Jem to walk through. Should she? Yes, she decided after a short deliberation. It might help to forestall future questions. If Cassie had been wondering, Jadine probably was, too.

Jem took a bite, chewed slowly. What to say?

Certainly nothing about two freakishly high cash cards and a hand comp holding a scientific bombshell. Or about Kurzvall and his watchers. She'd been dodging them for the past week. As unwanted as it was, Jem had to admit her mutation came in handy at times. An advantage she was loathe to use any more than absolutely necessary. Organ failure could be dealt with medically. The specter of being stuck in a *phased* limbo or a psych ward was what haunted her dreams.

Taking a sip of her water, Jem cleared her throat. "I recently lost several friends. The Myerstone explosion?" Cassie's eyes widened, filling with sympathy. "I worked there this past summer. One of them, Christine…we got to be good friends." Swallowing, she looked down, the sudden shaft of pain unexpected. Guess she hadn't come to terms with their deaths yet.

"I'm so sorry, Jem. Have you talked to anyone about it? A professional?" Cassie asked gently. "I can't image grieving for seven people."

Six. She wasn't about to grieve for Neal Grathen. Recovered DNA evidence from Myerstone had listed his name with the others. From

Kurzvall's outburst, she'd already known he hadn't survived Dougson that night.

"I had a hard time with *one*," Cassie continued, "when my grandpa died two years ago. For months, I just went through the motions of living. Having your place broken into last week probably hasn't helped. Have the Enforcers come up with anything yet?"

"No." Jem replied, guilt flitting through her.

Both floors of Mr. Petrov's home had been ransacked. He had lost several valuable antique heirlooms that had been in his family for generations. Those had probably been a bonus, as it would be highly coincidental if it hadn't been Kurzvall's men looking for the hand comp. It was safely hidden in an airport locker, since she'd kind of been expecting it. She hadn't expected her landlord's things to be taken, which had been a dumb oversight. A robbery was the perfect cover for any home break-in.

Cassie reached over and patted her hand. "If you need help kickstarting your life again, I can give you a name—he helped me more than I can ever say."

Jem gave the woman a wan smile. "Thanks. It's getting better," she replied, "but I'll keep your offer in mind. I saw those huge purple flowers that came in this morning. What are they and who's the lucky bride?"

They spent the rest of lunch talking flowers, floral arrangements, and the persnickety demands of brides and their mothers.

***

Later that evening, Jem sipped on Moon Ale and thought about what little she'd accomplished in the past weeks. Looking up an old acquaintance of Dani and Sam's had been the highlight. Raj No-Last-Name had raised an eyebrow but didn't ask any questions as he carefully cut the tracker band off her leg. Considering that and his offer to provide everything needed for an alias, she idly wondered where and how her friends had met him.

Otherwise? Yeah, she'd simply been going through the motions. Working, playing hide-and-seek with Kurzvall's goons. Waiting for LE to come knocking at her door. Having both the cash and Myerstone data in her possession, she'd half-expected Kurzvall to accuse *her* of what Neal Grathen had done and then of extorting money from him.

Jem sighed, rubbed her neck. She'd left Myerstone to take charge of her life. It was time to get off her butt and do so. Okay, first item. How to minimize that risk from Law Enforcement?

She left a bit early the next morning, having decided to deposit those insane cash cards into her bank account on her way to work. Grathen hadn't been kidding about being rich. She hadn't realized a card could hold that many credits. She'd swear the ATM had 'burped' on the second one.

Now, what to do about the data on the hand comp? *Hmmm.*

Jem pondered on it when not chatting with customers or ringing up sales. By suppertime, she'd settled on renting storage space at one of the major computer firms. She'd upload the data then wipe the hand comp. Then paranoia reared its head. Think about a bored, unethical technician browsing through server files, it warned. They could probably understand enough of the information to realize it was worth a lot. And to the man whose name was featured prominently, if unflatteringly, in a number of the team's personal memos and emails Grathen had copied.

Nope. Not worth the risk. Next idea?

At 0320 the next morning, her eyes popped open and she sat straight up in bed. The comp and the data it held were actually two different components. She could give Kurzvall the first while withholding the second. What a fantastic idea. Thank you, hindbrain, or Universe, or whatever spirit had whispered in her ear. Wide awake, Jem rolled out of bed.

It took two days to come up with what Jem considered a viable plan.

Mr. Petrov's heirlooms had taught her a valuable lesson. She had to consider the whole picture, think through all the possible ramifications, especially concerning people. She was a veritable lightning rod of bad luck to those around her. Nothing was beyond the two SOBs, and they didn't care who got hurt while doing it.

She was going to give the hand comp back to Kurzvall, after locking it with a passcode. Passcodes were an extremely secure way to protect something, as imputing the wrong one, or trying to hack it, would result in an unsalvageable mess. For additional security, she'd also encrypt its data. She had thought about placing an anonymous call to the authorities after he had it, but decided against it. Too risky. Kurzvall could spin it any number of ways, most likely it being what she'd been afraid of: him accusing her of doing Grathen's deeds. Her word against his and with no evidence to back up what really happened? And her recent huge deposit? *Uh-huh. Know the ending to that scenario.*

She called Detective Alfred LeBlanc, asking him the status of his Myerstone investigation.

"With no sign of any kind of explosive material or chemical compounds, we're closing it as a catastrophic but unknown failure in their manipulation of the Otanak and whatever other fields they were messing with. No offense to your friends," he said, "but that first explosion in December should have been a warning."

"It was. They spent months researching. But…guess things just happen." *Or someone helps them along.*

"True. It'll take about a week for my case report to be filed," he said. "It has to go through various offices for review and final approval."

"I'm looking at taking a job elsewhere. Is it okay for me to leave?" Jem asked.

"Sure. No need to hang around for the paperwork."

Jem thanked him and hung up. While she didn't have a specific job in mind, she definitely knew it wouldn't be on Earth. Once Kurzvall found the comp's contents were locked tight, he'd be after her in earnest. Nowhere would be safe, not with his money and resources.

"Jem Seaborne Wilmont! You're wanting to drift through space? Like some comet?"

Jem smiled ruefully at the memory. She'd told Dani she was thinking about heading off-world as they loaded mail pods that fateful day. It was no longer an option now.

Chapter 12

Jem gave a one-week notice to her employer the next morning, then fielded questions from Cassie all day. Mr. Petrov didn't even try to hide his dismay when she told him the same that evening.

"I've enjoyed my stay, truly," she told him. "But this was only meant to be short-term."

"Any reason you can't make it long-term?" he rebutted crossly.

Jem laughed, explaining she had 'wandering feet,' as Ned had put it. She accepted his offer of supper and they played a game of chess afterward. She would miss him, Jem thought, making her way upstairs.

She waited two more days before sneaking into Reginald Kurzvall's hotel suite late at night. Assuming he'd be in bed, she planned to leave the hand comp laying on that side table he'd smacked into. He'd assume she had snuck in using a combination of her 'security skills' and invisibility. Well, she thought crossly, that had been the plan.

Kurzvall was in the middle of a very heated video comp call.

Standing not two meters from him, she listened as he berated someone…in the Federal Senate? *Oh, my.*

"I expect positive action on this issue," Kurzvall snapped. "If you can't handle it, I'll make sure your replacement can."

"Mr. Kurzvall, I assure you—"

Kurzvall terminated the call and turned to a tall, slender man standing off to the side. "McNeil, I want the name of every person sitting on that incompetent's committees—Judicial and Appropriations especially."

Jem frowned. An aide? He hadn't been here the night she was kidnapped. Not wanting to come back later, she was debating where to leave the hand comp. The aide would have the bedroom, so… *The couch looks high enough. I can leave it under there and then call and tell him where it is. Have him wonder when I put it there.*

Jem was almost to the couch when the table comp signaled another message. Curious, she paused to listen as Kurzvall activated it. Another Federal Senator? Her amusement slid into shock at the recorded audio message.

"Meridan System assignment is complete. Planetary Representative Ben Webley has been eliminated in a staged accident as per your preference. Awaiting final payment as agreed. End."

"Excellent," Kurzvall said, his tone satisfied.

Jem stared, too stunned to even curse.

Rising, Kurzvall ordered his aide to pull the mercenary's final payment from their special account, then contact Dougson to arrange delivery of the cash card. Adding, "I'm going to bed. You can leave when that's done." He walked down a short hallway and into what was probably the master bedroom.

She stood there, trying to process all she'd heard. Unbelievable. LE sure wouldn't believe her if she tried to tell them. What the *hell* was Kurzvall involved in? By now, the aide was sitting in the comp niche, but he was fiddling with his hand comp. She went and peeked over his shoulder as he laid it down next to him. It displayed a file with—*wow*—a lot of accounts and their passwords. Some to banks here on Earth, but most of them off-world. Kurzvall's business interests appeared to be all over the Republic.

McNeil brought up the home page for First Federated Systems Bank on the local network and carefully input his information. The account summary page appeared and Jem's mouth dropped open at the information displayed.

"McNeil!" Kurzvall called.

The man's jaw tightened, but he immediately got up and walked down the hall. Leaving everything open.

The password she could remember. The fact she agreed heartily with his mnemonics about his boss helped. But that long account number? Taking a risk, Jem moved out of view of the hall and materialized. Acting quickly, she accessed the menu and had a copy of the summary emailed to her then closed the account to hide the action. She *shifted* about four seconds before McNeil came around the corner. *Whew.*

He sat down, then gave an annoyed grunt. He logged back into the bank account.

Leaving him to do whatever, Jem stuck her head through the door leading into the bedroom she'd escaped from. Nope, the aide wasn't using it. Kurzvall's preference or McNeil's? She'd certainly prefer to sleep elsewhere. *Phasing* all the way into the room, Jem held the comp slightly above the bed and released it. Watched it materialize and drop with an unsettled feeling drawing her stomach muscles tight. That feature of *phasing*, so full of negative implications, had strengthened her resolve to keep her ability secret. She *phased* out of the bedroom and was half-way to the hallway wall when Kurzvall reappeared, wearing a silky-looking bathrobe.

"Has a message come in from Senator Bernhagen yet?" he snapped.

Did the man not ever sleep? Jem hesitated. She was probably nearing her limit, but… What would she hear this time?

"Yes," McNeil said, checking the comp's email function. "A text message."

"Read it."

"Mr. Kurzvall, I have taken your proposition under advisement and believe that your idea can be accommodated. I will need to make certain arrangements on this end that might prove costly."

Kurzvall snorted. "Naturally. And the bastard will take his percentage. Continue."

Jem's lips pursed as she listened. An under-the-table contract-fixing scheme with an Orion System Senator. Why was she not surprised? *Oh, oh.* That warning tug meant she was about to be yanked back to reality.

She made a mad dash through the wall and down the hotel corridor to the stairwell. She knew from her last 'visit' there were no cameras there.

***

Jem purchased four cash cards on her way to work the next morning, from four different stores to prevent any rampant speculation. Although buying the largest size available had raised two sets of eyebrows. Antsy, impatient, she'd managed to act normally throughout the workday. Well, maybe not completely. She'd caught Cassie eyeing her once or twice.

Now, safely tucked into her room, she brought up the bank's log-on page on the computer. Carefully, she entered Kurzvall's account number, then the password: regKurzUn1ver*e#1b@st@rd. She felt a pang of sympathy for McNeil. He couldn't walk away, not with what he knew about Kurzvall and his activities. His fate was sealed: another *accident* sooner or later. And he had to know it.

When the account menu came up, she clicked on the 'Withdrawal' option and plugged the first card into the port. Jem selected 'Fill Card', hit 'Enter', and leaned back in her chair. Thank goodness Mr. Petrov had outfitted the apartment with top quality electronics after deciding to rent out his second floor. Withdrawing as large an amount as she was might have caused problems using one of the bank's self-service machines. Like halting the action and requesting additional verification that she didn't have. While it was still possible, the odds were a lot less this way.

A box displaying "Completed" popped up onscreen. Jem nearly

choked at the amount shown downloaded. Evidently Grathen's cards hadn't been the biggest available. Removing the full card, she inserted a second one. Ten minutes later, she had three stuffed cash cards and Kurzvall's special account was down to thirteen credits. Grinning, she logged out of the account. She'd return the unopened fourth card for a refund.

Jem glanced at the clock. Okay. Next step. The hotel connected her video call to the table comp in Kurzvall's room. The aide answered. She waited while he went to check the bedroom.

"Why?" McNeil asked when he returned, voice and expression both puzzled.

"Why return it? So that your manipulative, murderous boss can't accuse me of what he had Neal Grathen do," Jem told him coldly. "However, that doesn't mean he gets its contents."

He looked down, then back up. "It's passcoded?"

"Uh-huh."

Silence. In a low voice, McNeil said, "Run, fast and far." The call ended.

Well, that was interesting. If there ever was anything she could do to help him, she would. Now, what to do with enough credits to buy several star-class luxury liners?

Chapter 13

She should have taken McNeil's warning to heart.

Jem was making her way up the sidewalk the next evening. She'd spent an hour after work at the hospital, visiting Cassie and her newborn twins. They'd arrived a bit early, as twins had a tendency to do. They were pronounced as healthy by the doctor and 'perfect' by their father.

Jem was hunched into a jacket that didn't do much to block the sharp wind blowing. It was already dark, courtesy of the heavy overcast that heralded an early winter. She was passing the small playground three houses down from Mr. Petrov's when three men exploded from two cars parked at the curb. One was Dougson.

With no time for her to do anything more than suck in a breath, Dougson fired. The stun shot hit her in the chest. One of his men grabbed her from behind to catch her as she collapsed. Except she didn't. Jem blinked, seeing the same astonishment in Dougson's face that she was feeling, along with a prickly sensation spreading through her torso. Recovering, she shoved both elbows into the stomach of the guy holding her. Got a grunt. Got a *bitch* when she slammed her foot down on one of his. Desperate, Jem twisted in his hold. The other guy was closing in on her and she couldn't fight both.

Suddenly, Mr. Petrov was barreling down the sidewalk toward them, brandishing the old-fashioned shotgun the robbers had missed.

"Let her go—enforcers are coming!" he yelled.

"No!" Jem screamed as both Dougson and the third guy fired. *Z-ping, z-ping.*

A guy from the closest house stepped out and yelled, "What the hell is go—*z-ping*." A stunner shot dropped him.

Jem twisted again, breaking free from the distracted thug's grasp. Running, she sank down next to Mr. Petrov's collapsed form. Behind her, Dougson was cursing loudly as sirens sounded nearby. Car doors slammed and, tires screeching, they bolted.

***

Jem stared blankly at a wall in the hospital's waiting room. Numb.

"Miss Wilmont?"

Her gaze traveled slowly to the man in front of her. It wasn't until he was seated beside her that she recalled his name.

"Detective LeBlanc?" She looked around; no sign of the female detective that had questioned her earlier.

"Detective Poe called me," he said.

"Why?" Jem asked dully.

"She ran a check through our database. This is the third incident in four weeks that your name has been attached to. A sequence of incidents that are…interesting."

Jem's brain-fog popped like a balloon. The tone might have been bland, but it didn't mask the suspicion in his sharp eyes.

"You worked at Myerstone, fortuitously leaving before its destruction, then your residence is ransacked, and now a public assault. How is Mr. Petrov?"

Jem swallowed and looked away. "He died. Just a little bit ago."

The doctor's voice had been gentle; the news had been hard. Mr. Petrov had only been in his late seventies, but had a weak heart. Two stun shots to the chest had been too much for it. *Damn them. Damn Dougson and Kurzvall both.*

Silence. "My condolences," LeBlanc finally said. "You have no idea who they were or why they assaulted you, according to Detective Poe."

Miserable. Tired. Jem turned to him. "I'm sorry, Detective," she said. "I'm not up to answering questions tonight. Tomorrow would be better."

"Perhaps it would be," he said agreeably. "Where will you be staying?"

Jem flinched. She just couldn't…not there. "Transit hotel. I'll come to the Law Enforcement Center in the morning."

"I can offer you a ride, if you're ready to leave. Any injuries needing attention yourself?"

She shook her head. Her injury was to her soul. Kurzvall had moved way faster than she had anticipated. *Just a few more days, was that too much to ask?* she bitterly demanded of the universe. Then she would have been gone and Mr. Petrov would still be alive.

Detective LeBlanc drove her to Mr. Petrov's home so she could get her things. He even went in with her to 'insure it was safe.' She didn't have a lot and most of it was already in her travel bag. Ensuring LeBlanc's attention was in the main room, she loosened the three cash cards taped to the underside of the night table and packed them along with the rest of her things. Jem gave a final look around; she wouldn't be coming back.

LeBlanc dropped her off at the transit hotel she'd stayed at previously.

A week passed. Jem lied to the Enforcers, lied to Cassie and Jadine, lied to Ned and Janet, who'd made a beeline for her hotel after they'd learned what had happened. Mr. Petrov's house had been closed up, his lawyer taking control of his estate. Otherwise, it was uneventful. The enforcers watching outside the hotel and trailing her when she went out probably had a lot to do with that. Detectives Poe and LeBlanc knew she was withholding information, but couldn't do anything without proof. They were watching, waiting for something else to happen.

Jem fervently wished Dougson would try something. Anything.

Unfortunately for them all, 'dumb' wasn't on her list of descriptors for him.

Then came a knock on her door. She opened it, then gaped at the hostile, younger image of Mr. Petrov in an Army uniform.

"May I come in?"

"Oh. Please. Sorry, it's just that…you look so much like your father."

"The man killed because of you?"

Jem flinched.

"I've spoken with the enforcers. My father's case will soon go into the cold drawer due to lack of clues or progress. I got the impression that it was more than an attempted robbery gone bad. Then me and Detective LeBlanc had a private chat, and your name figured prominently in that conversation."

Jem's chin came up as he took a threatening step forward.

"What are you involved in? What did my father really die for?"

"Your father was trying to stop the men who ambushed me."

"Who and why?"

"I don't know."

"Lie," he snarled, so viciously Jem took a step back. "I *know* a lie when I hear it."

Great. A human lie detector. She'd met one in Ireland. Jem studied him for a moment, seeing the determination in that hard gaze. Mr. Petrov's son was owed more than lies. However, intuition told her that if she gave him the whole truth, he'd ruin his career, maybe his life, trying to get justice. Or revenge.

"Why don't we have a seat—sorry, I don't recognize your rank."

"Sergeant Major Jonathan McCaul Petrov."

Jem sat across from him. "Your father was very proud of you, you know," she said in a reminiscing voice. "He showed me the picture of you and him, celebrating your graduation from Army Ranger school."

His reply was a hard, cold glare.

Jem chewed her lip. Screw it. "Between us? On your word?"

"On my word," he replied, touching the stripes on his left sleeve with three fingers.

"Yes, I've withheld information and told a few lies." *Few?* "There's a reason I can't give you or the enforcers what you want. It's complicated, and the stakes…are too high."

"You're undercover Fed? Military?" he said sharply.

"No, just a civilian that got caught up in…something. Your father…" Jem looked away for several seconds, fought and won the battle against tears. "Believe me, his death…and others…weigh on me."

Understanding dawned in his eyes. "Myerstone?"

Jem swallowed, nodded. "Maybe someday I can say more. But not now. It would endanger others. You."

The silence lasted between them for several minutes. Sergeant Major Petrov stood.

"My father's memorial is in two days. We'd both be pleased to have you there." He walked to the door, paused and faced back toward her. "Watch your back."

***

The memorial was a small affair at Mr. Petrov's home. There wasn't a large crowd, as many of his friends and acquaintances had preceded him in death. A picture of him and his deceased wife leaned against the urn holding both their ashes, as per his will. Jem sat in the back row, listening as they reminisced and smiling at their anecdotes. She wasn't surprised to learn Mr. Petrov had been quite the character in his younger days. When it appeared to be winding down, Jem slipped quietly out the door.

Sergeant Major Petrov had never glanced her way, maintaining the cold-shoulder distance the Enforcers that were watching expected. Had they stopped him, questioned him about their meeting? If so, he had indeed kept their confidence.

She walked, not caring where her feet took her. Or that the cold, fine mist was slowly soaking her jacket. She thought of her friends, of that Planetary Representative who'd been killed. How many others? Kurzvall's hands were just as bloody as the ones who executed his orders. No, bloodier. Angry determination settled like a cloak over her shoulders. It seeped into her bones. Law Enforcement couldn't do anything, but she could. They'd need evidence, proof of his crimes. She'd seen and heard them first-hand. Experienced them.

She vowed to become an invisible thorn in his ass, in any way that she could find.

Chapter 14

Jem studied the outbound board. She'd taken the first shuttle to the Mobile Spaceport as soon as Mr. Petrov's case went into the cold drawer and she was free to travel. There—passage to Mars City was leaving in one hour, ten minutes. Having only a travel bag and backpack, she skipped the main counter and headed to one of the kiosks.

Flight 34001…Ugh. No seats available. The computer helpfully informed her of available seats on a flight leaving in nine hours. She didn't want to wait. The longer she remained here, the more risk that Dougson would find her. She didn't want any more deaths on her conscience. She queried the computer for all destinations with available seats leaving in… Jem thought for a moment, then went with four hours.

Coleman Two, Euphrates One, Zepher Five, Hallmark Three, Wotan Two…Jem sighed. Planning on going to Mars City, she hadn't researched any other planets' gravity, economics, or types of industries. No time now. Her gaze landed on Fulbright Space Station, Taurus System, near the bottom of the screen. It was the second stop by *Cosmic Trails,* leaving in three hours, ten minutes, and with shuttles starting forty minutes prior. Okay, that should be a safe first step. Space stations usually maintained Earth Standard gravity and there should be service jobs available.

Jem was careful to stay in crowded places. She enjoyed a surprisingly good Reuben sandwich in the Food Court. Then she took a port runner to Terminal Three and had a long walk down to Gate 43C. It was standing room only. *Wow.* No wonder the few remaining tickets had been in the multi-bunk economy rooms. Jem managed to squeeze into a spot while they all waited for shuttles to deliver them to the liner in orbit. She tried—nonchalantly—to keep watch for anyone paying her too much attention.

Being squished in the back of the room, Jem was on the last shuttle landing in the Star Cruiser's small shuttle bay. The head steward greeted them with an automatic smile as they disembarked. Not yet ready to find her room, she handed her travel bag with its room tag to one of his helpers and made her way to the lounge. Other passengers with the same idea already half-filled it.

The large viewscreen on one wall displayed the turning Earth beneath them. The vast blueness of the Pacific Ocean was visible below white strips of clouds. North America was just vanishing around the curvature. Home. This was her first time leaving it. Longing became a vise clamped around her heart. When would she walk its land again? Breathe its air? *One day*, she promised herself, *I'll return when it's safe.*

Safe. Right, some pessimistic part of her brain snarked.

Nowhere was safe, on or off Earth, as long as Kurzvall stalked her, she now realized. She'd researched him and his business interests while waiting for clearance to leave. Kurzvall Industries, as shown by McNeil's password file, was an enormous conglomerate with parts scattered all over the Republic. Undoubtedly with puppets on those worlds, dancing to his commands if his manipulation of Federation Senators was any indication. Which meant those around her wouldn't be safe either.

No one, Jem vowed, *no one else would suffer because of her.*

The announcements started. Captain Katherine Moser gave them the expected "Welcome aboard *Cosmic Trails*" speech, followed by general ship information by someone whose name she'd missed, too focused on the changing image on the viewscreen as the ship got under way. Its ion engines would take them out of the Earth-Moon gravitational field before the Otanak engine would be activated.

Only half-listening, Jem's thoughts turned inward.

She'd deposited the three cash cards into her account yesterday after her watchers were withdrawn. A low laugh escaped, imagining the bank employees' faces when they'd reviewed the end-of-day transactions. She had debated what to do with all those credits, but eventually her unknown future won out over charities. Granted, her account had already been well padded with Grathen's two cards, but there was no telling what she might run into. What her thorn-in-the-Kurzvall-butt plans might need, especially if it meant buying information from some low-life. All of which could be expensive. Which is why she'd only discarded two of the cards afterwards, keeping one for any large credit transactions in her future. Besides, using those tainted funds against him just seemed like karma.

Earth continued to dwindle; the moon peeked from a top corner.

The plan she'd decided on was simple. She'd become one of those cosmic drifters, moving between star systems and working low-level jobs. Hanging around Port Circles with no sign of income and for no apparent reason would quickly draw unwanted attention. She'd never stay long enough for Kurzvall's hunters to find her and leave with little-to-no notice in case they did. Her mistake in giving her enemies time to act had cost Mr. Petrov his life. Blue-colored eye contacts she'd purchased a couple of days ago currently hid her most distinctive feature. Defensive training was high on her priority list. Dougson and his goons would use brute force the next time since she was apparently immune to stunners now.

Dammit. She really was a freak. *Anything else?* she bitterly asked the universe as a double chime over the loudspeaker signaled transition to O-space, the unknown dimension the Otanak engine drove them through.

The viewscreen went black and a throbbing started at the base of her neck. *No, no, no.* Hadn't O-fields messed her life up enough? Now she had to *feel* the damn thing? *Go away!*

But the throbbing beat steadily, almost like a second heartbeat. Jem let out a tired sigh. She just had to ask, didn't she? Teach her to taunt the universe again. What other frigging surprises did her mutated body hide? She rubbed her eyes. Sleep. She needed sleep. Between nightmares of the hanger, Myerstone, and Mr. Petrov, she rarely slept a whole night anymore. Maybe she could ask the ship's medic for something.

Jem pushed up from the table, grabbed her backpack and headed for room seventy-one. She hoped none of her five roommates snored.

Chapter 15

The Fulbright Space Station was an older construct. The public concourse and business areas had managed to spiff themselves up, but its age was evident in the narrow corridors, harsh lighting, and outdated features. And expensive. She was paying triple the rate for half the size of her hotel room back on Earth. Many of her coworkers here had doubled up to reduce expenses.

She was in her third week on the station, sipping on Moon Ale and brooding in a back corner of *Blooming Spirits*, a misnomer of a name if there ever was. Nothing bloomed down in this section of the station except apathy and desperation. A couple more weeks and she'd be just like the rest of them.

Mopping floors, emptying trashcans, and cleaning restrooms wasn't the worst job she'd had—that belonged to cleaning out a Scottish farmer's pig pen after losing a bet, although the men's restroom down in Eight-E might run a close second. It was barely making enough to cover those expenses that was the problem. Anything extra, like Moon Ale, was gradually whittling down her cash card. She'd filled it before leaving Earth and still had plenty, but at this rate…maybe she shouldn't have totally emptied that cash card of Kurzvall's she'd kept.

Of course, she could always request a fund transfer from her Earth account through the station's finance office. Wouldn't that raise a few eyebrows? And suspicions? Could Kurzvall's resources somehow trace it?

That thought sent a chill racing down her spine. No, she'd wait a bit longer.

Jem glanced up briefly when Station Security Chief Jay Tatarenko walked in.

On top of it all, Jem fretted into her glass, she missed Earth. Missed the sky, missed the starry nights, missed the frigging fresh air. They really, really needed to update the station's circulation system. *No way I can stay another*—Jem blinked in surprise when Chief Tatarenko sat down across from her.

"Jem Seaborne Wilmont, right?"

"Yes, sir," she replied warily. Not that she'd done anything wrong. Lately.

"Officer Waite's report states that you accessed Supply Two, in Section Five-F two days ago. You overheard Pauline Christiansen in a heated argument with a man before you withdrew. You're sure it was her?"

Ah, he was investigating the woman's murder. Her body had been found later that same night in Two's maintenance locker, her skull's right side caved in. Officers had spent most of yesterday interviewing everyone she worked with or lived in the same corridor. Or, in Jem's case, having been identified as being in the murder vicinity, courtesy of the chip in her staff ID card. Access to all employee-only and station-controlled areas were recorded in an audit file. The officer interviewing her had spent a good fifteen minutes asking questions from every angle after she'd mentioned the argument.

"Yes, I'm pretty good with voices. Living several doors down from me, I'd heard her a number of times." Loudly. Anticipating the next questions, she continued. "No, I didn't recognize the man's voice. And no, I didn't hang around. I backed out as soon as I heard them." She had gone down to get supplies for her janitorial cart.

"The only entries recorded for Supply Two between 1305 and the discovery of the body at 1846 were Miss Christiansen at 1632 and you twice, at 1649 and 1731. Time of death is estimated at 1700…give or take," he said in a neutral tone.

She stiffened. That explained Officer Waite's suspicious questions. "If you think I killed her, why aren't you interrogating me up in Security?" Jem asked bluntly. Her pulse rate picked up as the Chief stared at her in silence.

Well, crap. That might be exactly why he was here.

Finally, "According to medical, her skull was crushed with significant force by a blunt object yet to be found. Forensics has scoured Supply Two, that whole section, and the supply cart you were using that day. They can't find any blood or hair traces other than at the murder scene. Your next logged position after 1649 is only fourteen minutes, twenty-two seconds later in a Five-D employee lounge, which is at least a ten-minute walk from Supply Two, especially pushing a cart. Doesn't leave a lot of time to kill and hide Christiansen's body before heading to the lounge. Nor are there any reports of a janitorial cart racing through Five's corridors." A smile came and went unexpectedly.

Jem rolled her eyes and relaxed.

"So no, I don't think you are the killer. It was undoubtedly an arranged rendezvous and he entered along with Pauline Christiansen. He either went there planning to kill her or lost his temper and lashed out using something close to hand. You did say the argument was heated. Any idea what it was about?" he added.

Jem's lips pursed, causing his gaze to sharpen. Well, the woman was beyond embarrassment. "Sounded like they were arguing over her rates. He said she wasn't worth more than what he was already paying her. That's why I left and hit the vending machine in the lounge. Not a voyeur." It wasn't the first time she'd interrupted a heavy lip-lock or other "activity." She continued with, "The supplies I needed were on shelves on the opposite side of the room from the murder scene, so I didn't notice anything when I went back about thirty, forty minutes later." She'd ended up being chewed out by her supervisor for checking her cart in late.

Tatarenko stared at her for several seconds, then glanced casually around the room. There was no one at the nearby tables. "Would you recognize the man's voice if you heard it again?" he asked, lowering his voice.

"Sure," Jem said, shrugging. "But how likely is it he's the murderer? If he was unhappy with her, he could just stop, uh, seeing her. Sex isn't worth killing for." She raised her glass.

"No," he said softly, "but two kilos worth of drugs is."

The ale went down the wrong pipe. "Drugs?" Jem managed to wheeze out between coughs.

"Prepackaged units, ready to distribute." He looked around again. "Christiansen worked here as a cargo handler for three years, the perfect position to intercept something not on the manifest. Considering the timing, what we found hidden in her room was probably from a supply ship that went through here a week ago. I've ordered that information kept quiet."

"Then why are you telling me?"

Tatarenko leaned forward, a hard glint in his dark brown eyes. "I have a murderer on station. Worse, I have a drug dealer here, too. A piece of shit that can be identified by *you*, simply by hearing him speak. In that respect, I'd like for you to wander around the station, hit all the public areas. Bars, restaurants, browse the shops."

Jem stared at him for several seconds, aghast. "Do you know how long that could take, what the odds are? Where to even start?"

"We know he doesn't work anywhere in the supply system or he wouldn't have needed Pauline Christiansen. Hence, concentrating on the public areas."

"What if he leaves in the meantime?"

The Chief's smile held no humor. "Short term, I can lock the station down, prohibit any passage off. However, I doubt our guy will do anything so blatantly obvious."

"Tell you what," Jem said sourly, "why don't you line all the men up and have them each say a line or two."

His right eyebrow popped upward. "Not a bad idea, but impractical."

"Not as much as yours," she shot back.

"And when he realizes we have a way to voice ID him?"

Jem's mouth hung open for a beat, then she opted for a gulp of ale.

Tatarenko tapped the table, then quietly admitted, "I'm worried, Miss Wilmont. Worried that he'll bide his time, then restart *business* when he feels it safe. Fulbright Station, like everywhere else, has drug issues. Ours has been a relatively small problem, despite a recent uptick in both drug related arrests and medical cases. But this…this is a massive escalation and undoubtedly why Christiansen got greedy. I'm hazarding she wanted a larger cut and refused to relinquish the product until she got it."

"Then killing her was stupid. He should have waited until after he got the drugs from her, considering all the possible hiding places."

"Which points to the lost temper scenario. Hiding it in her room was brilliant, as that'd be the most obvious and therefore the last place someone would look."

Tatarenko leaned back and locked Jem's gaze with his own. "I want to find him, Miss Wilmont. I want to stomp out this filth before it takes hold, before it devastates lives. I'll investigate all avenues, use any and all resources to find this guy."

Including you, his eyes told her.

Jem understood his drive. Understood the horrors rooted in drugs. Like a drug-crazed addict with a metal-tipped bat, screaming about monsters as he attacked an elementary school playground filled with kids.

Teachers batted aside with adrenaline-hyped strength as they tried to stop him or shield children. By the time Enforcers arrived, his score was twenty-eight wounded and seven dead. Dani's Sam and three children were among the latter.

Tatarenko couldn't force her to help; he didn't need to. She'd do it for her lost friends, for all the lost innocents and those endangered. "I agree wholeheartedly," Jem simply said. "I'll do what I can."

"Thank you," Tatarenko said, a smile briefly lighting his face. "I'll keep the fact you can identify him to myself. Contact me directly, even if you're not one hundred percent positive it's him." Appropriating Jem's napkin, he wrote his comm number on it. Slid it back across. "Watch your back," he said, before walking away.

Huh. The exact same warning Sergeant Major Petrov had given her.

Chapter 16

For a week, Jem spent her off-duty hours sipping drinks at bars, eating at various food outlets, browsing through stores, and generally wandering up and down the concourse. Nothing. When she stepped out of *Quittin' Time* well after midnight, she looked at the bar's sign and agreed. Her bed was calling her.

Finding a small crowd waiting at the elevator, she plopped down on a nearby bench. She was tired, running short on sleep, and watching her cash balance drop. Massaging her neck, Jem wondered if Tatarenko would slip her some credits if she asked. This was his idea, after all.

The elevator dinged. Jem leaned back, eyes closed, too tired to move. She'd catch the next one. Then came a booming laugh, followed by, "No problem. I'll see what I can do."

Him! Jem sprang up and whipped around—as the elevator doors closed. The oversized elevator carriage had inhaled all of them. *Dammit!* Teeth gritted, Jem barely managed to hold back a frustrated scream as she watched the upward pointing indicator. Mentally counting the seconds, she was unsurprised at the time it took before switching to a downward arrow.

Naturally, she groused, *why should my luck get any better.*

It had stopped at most of—if not all—the three levels above the Concourse. When its doors opened, only two women got off. Jem boarded with the other late-nighters that had gathered. She recognized two that lived in the same corridor as her, supporting a very drunk third. Fortunately, no one selected an upper level and the elevator continued downward. Most of them exited on residential Level Seven with her. From the glum faces on the two that didn't, Jem figured they were headed for an it-can't-wait job on Eight, the maintenance level.

Discouraged, feet and spirits dragging, Jem headed for her room. While she was tempted to get the Security Chief out of his comfy, warm bed, it'd serve no purpose. Other than a bit of petty revenge, maybe. She'd call him in the morning.

***

Oversleeping, late for work, Jem was on her lunch hour before she got a chance to call Chief Tatarenko. He was thrilled she could positively recognize the voice, not so thrilled at the lack of physical identification. Jem could see the same frustration in his face that she was feeling.

"Where are you?"

"My quarters. Didn't think you'd want this conversation at a public comm." His grunt was probably agreement.

"You don't have *any* description?"

"No. I was beat and nearly falling asleep on my feet," she replied, a bit testy. She'd already apologized for not giving more attention to the crowd. It'd been totally unexpected.

He held up a placating hand. "Understood. At least our search is narrowed down a bit."

Really? "How do you figure that?"

"Obviously, he's a night-worker. While there are other offices, including those with round-the-clock services, the functions on those levels are primarily Medical, Operations, and Security."

Silence, as each of them thought that over.

"Medical," Jem finally said, "would know all about drugs. Maybe have some dubious contacts."

"True, but anyone could have those. The other two…" He paused. "Operations covers the station's infrastructure, funds, and ship schedules. The high end. Security covers everything happening on the station. The low end. If he set up a monitoring program on the station network with specific search parameters, he'd know everything. And probably has," Tatarenko bit out. "It would explain why we've been unable to make any progress on that front."

He vented with several cuss words. "There were rumors about a new drug pipeline five months ago, and we identified a suspect. Then he was killed in a suspiciously freak accident before we could arrest him. Dammit, I'm not going to be able to launch an investigation…make any move without him knowing it. Hell, he could be one of my officers."

"Can't a monitoring program be set up from anywhere?"

Tatarenko nodded. "But it'd be easier to sneak an unregistered program into the network from a terminal in one of those areas—they have higher and broader access permissions. Especially in Security. Unfortunately, it'll be invisible to our audit programs."

Jem gave him a crooked smile. "Guess it's a good thing you've kept me undercover." Tatarenko's eyes flicked sideways in the silence. "Haven't you?"

"Yes, but I've been monitoring your movements," he said apologetically.

Her lips pursed. "My *movements*? Not just recording area access?"

"We have a surveillance program that will pinpoint your card's location at any given moment."

"In other words, tracking me," Jem said, her tone as cool as the look she gave him. Good thing she hadn't *shifted* lately. "How hard would it be for him to get that info?"

"Easily. Assuming the SOB *is* monitoring me and my investigation," Tatarenko all but growled. "I've recorded the reason as precautionary and referenced your report, leaving out the voice identification info. He shouldn't believe it's otherwise. However, there's still the possibility he won't want to risk you having heard more than what you provided to us. Patrols were alerted to keep an eye on you when you're in their area. Not constant, just checking occasionally," he added hastily, when Jem gave him the stink eye.

Okay, she'd give him that. She glanced at the comp screen's lower right corner. "I've got about ten minutes left. What do we do now? I can't exactly wander those levels, especially at night."

His gaze drifted off to the left for a moment. Then, "Let me think on it. Meet me tonight at *Meizhen's*, Section Four-B, 2100." The screen blanked.

Jem hoped Tatarenko planned on picking up the tab. Four-B was in the ritzy part of the Concourse. *Meizhen's*, huh. Been awhile since she'd had Asian cuisine. But why meet there, of all places?

***

"Why are we meeting here?" Jem asked. "The maître d' didn't want to let me in until I dropped your name." Her clothes were clean and even new-ish, but still several steps down from that worn by the diners looking askance as she passed them. The server who'd escorted her to the table had poured her glass of water with polite disdain before leaving. Snooty bunch.

She eyed the man across from her. Out of uniform, the security chief cut a rather dashing figure. He was wearing a deep green shirt that contrasted nicely with his bronze skin and brown eyes, while accenting a mass of shoulder-length white-blond hair.

"I thought it would establish my interest in you nicely. I hope you like Italian."

Her expression must have been hilarious.

Chuckling, he added in a lowered tone, "Why else would I escort you on an extended tour of the upper levels?"

Jem's brain kicked back in. Ah. That was genius, except for one thing. "Is that believable? From the scuttlebutt I've overheard about your recent breakup, I'm not your type." The gossipers were hashing all sorts of reasons for both it and Charles Stubbins's subsequent and rather hurried exit off the station. *Aaaand* off-limits from that flexed jaw and hooded gaze.

"Shall we order?" he said, picking up his menu.

That had Jem remembering his earlier comment. Picking up hers, a quick perusal showed he was right. "Italian? I was expecting Asian."

"The name can be misleading," he replied tonelessly. "But Josephine Meizhen is an accomplished Chef of Italian cuisine." He looked over the menu top at Jem. "And an ex-lover so, yes, it'll be believable."

Ooookay. Studying her dinner choices was probably the safest course for the moment. Considering the speed at which the waiter arrived, he must have been watching. No auto-menus for this place.

Jem selected the evening's special: Sausage/Beef/Penne Combo smothered in a spicy sauce, served with toasted whole green beans and a mixed green salad with House Meizhen dressing.

Tatarenko ordered the same, then added, "We'll have the *Peperonata Meizhen* as an appetizer, plus a bottle of the house Moscato."

The server applauded his choices, snuck a condescending smile in Jem's direction, and hurried off. Silence stretched long enough for their sizzling appetizer to arrive.

"Well," she said, trying to restart the conversation, "It'll be interesting to see how close to the real thing our meals are." He cocked an eyebrow. "Not insulting anything," she hurriedly added, halting the bite of Peperonata. "But out here, the flavor of available ingredients—like spices—can differ, especially if not actually procured from Earth."

"Your employment file states you're an Earth native," he said, his affable manner reinserting itself.

Technically that wasn't true. But having lived there since she was two, she figured it was close enough.

"Never been there myself," Tatarenko continued, eyeing her thoughtfully. "Have you been to Italy? The original one?"

She nodded. That last was a valid question, considering how many Earth names had been reused. Afterall, it was easier to recycle the old names than come up with a bunch of new ones.

The conversation flowed smoothly after that, his questions and her answers interspersed between bites. Jem declared the food was excellent, although there needed to be a warning about the pasta dish. Spicey did not begin to properly describe it, and he'd laughed as she guzzled down her water after her large first forkful. They finished with large servings of apple pie and the last of the wine.

Jem leaned back and gave a discreet burp. "I've really enjoyed this, Chief, both the dinner and the company."

"Ditto, and you'd better start calling me Jay, Jem." His burp wasn't quite as discreet. "Especially now that we're burp buddies in a budding relationship."

Laughter burst out of her, surprising Jem. *Must be the wine.*

"Why did you leave Earth?" he asked, his tone curious. "Run out of places to visit?"

Jem's smile slowly died, her gaze losing focus as she looked backward. "I lost several friends," she said, grief underscoring her words. "I…needed to be somewhere else." Refocusing, she gave him a wry smile. "Fulbright won the toss."

"I'm sorry." After a moment of silence, his tone changed from sympathetic to business. "It was around 0100 when you heard him, right?" Jay said, pulling out his phone to check the time. "It's almost 2300 now, so he should be at work."

Wow. A two-hour dinner. It hadn't seemed that long. Even better, Jay signaled their server and pulled out his card. Its two-toned coloration told her it was a bank card, pulling the payment straight from his local account. She'd had to set up one for her employee payments after being hired, but she was still using her plain black cash card.

Jem waited until they were out in the Concourse before asking their next move.

"Browse down the concourse," he replied. "I want to wait a bit before going upstairs, in case he's running late."

They stopped in front of a window displaying a selection of electronics.

"How late are you looking to do this?" she asked, gaze on the display. "I do work tomorrow, you know." They started walking again.

"We'll do one area at a time, starting with mine as that would be natural. If we—you strike out, we'll do a repeat tomorrow night. Dinner, then a tour of Operations. You're *very* interested in things," he said airily.

Jem snorted. "Assumptions being that you're at the top of the list?"

"Yep." He linked his arm through hers. Grinned. "After all, I am considered quite the catch."

"Uh-huh. If we do a repeat, I get to pick the next restaurant."

***

The next night they had dinner at *The Howling Monkey*, an upbeat restaurant in Four-D with an eclectic menu and where her clothes wouldn't raise eyebrows, although her dinner companion did. Jay's brows had done a bit of bouncing, too, after learning where they were eating. He'd ordered a gyro after she explained what it was. Working her way through a large bowl of chili and basket of rolls, Jem grinned when he ordered a second one.

Jay plugged his bank card into the auto-menu's payment slot when they finished. "Ready?"

Jem took a deep breath as the light flashed green. "Ready."

Their tour of Operations was as big a dud as Security had been. *Well, not true,* Jem mused as they made their way back to the Concourse. They'd managed to irritate the on-duty Senior Controller who'd had to escort them through the various offices. Sitting on a bench outside the Four-D elevators—the same ones that had started this—Jem pondered their next move. The last section, Medical? They weren't likely to allow a late-night tour, even by the station security chief.

Beside her, Jay gave a frustrated sigh. "We'll not get to roam Medical without a damn good reason. I can't think of one, can you?"

Jem shook her head. "If it helps, I don't think our guy is there anyway. Based on what you've told me, they'd have limited non-medical access into the station's network."

"So we've missed him," he grumped.

"It was kind of a wild shot anyway, Jay," Jem consoled him. "Insisting to speak with every person would have raised more than eyebrows. Not to mention, he could've been out on an errand or his night off."

"Or out on patrol," Jay muttered, resting both elbows on the bench top.

Her lips gave a sympathetic twist. That was his worst fear: a traitor among his security people. Lost in their own thoughts, they sat in comfortable silence. While not as crowded as in the 'day' hours, the Concourse was never empty. People streamed by them or collected in front of the elevators. They collected quite a few sideways glances, too.

A large yawn almost cracked Jem's jaw. "Okay, I'm done," she said, standing.

Jay's hand caught hers as he stood. "We'll have to come up with a different plan."

"Obviously," she said dryly. She wiggled her fingers, but he didn't let go.

In a low, lazy drawl, he said, "You know, Miss Wilmont, you and those eyes just might tempt me into making this relationship real." He kissed her forehead before turning and walking away.

Jem stared after him, flustered and flabbergasted. Then added red-faced when she noted the number of smirks in the elevator crowd. Jem stoically ignored them all the way to her room. Once there, she stared into the mirror above the small dresser. She'd stopped wearing the contacts during the second week here.

Second week? How long…crap. She'd been here a month. If Kurzvall hadn't figured out by now that she'd left Earth, he would soon. How wide a net could his resources spread?

She needed to leave. But would Jay let her? He wanted her help…and maybe more. Her pulse spiked. The kiss had been chaste, but she'd felt all the possibilities it offered. Her heart lurched. Possibilities that could never come to pass.

Chapter 17

Chief Jay Tatarenko sat at his desk, reading a report on his comp screen. His mind was only half on it; the other half was pondering what to do about their problem. Jem couldn't keep wandering the station, hoping for another fluke encounter like the one at the elevator. A Star Cruise liner was due in a couple of days. Freezing outbound ticket purchases—he could hear the complaints—would be a short-term stopgap. Unless the killer turned psycho and went on a rampage, he couldn't justify prohibiting the ones wanting to leave on the next transport.

He frowned off into space. Allow female ticket purchases but not male? No, the killer could have a female accomplice that could abscond with any materially incriminating evidence. It'd be highly unlikely they would get a conviction on just Jem's voice recognition. That merely placed him in Supply Two and having an argument. Nothing more.

His thoughts segued to Jem, to the enjoyable hours he'd spent with her, despite the unpleasant reason for doing so. She had a likable, good-natured personality and a wicked sense of humor that hid an acute intelligence. He'd been surprised at some of the insightful questions she'd asked during their 'tours.' And those eyes? Besides just plain fascinating, he was curious about the wariness he occasionally glimpsed in them. No, he wouldn't mind spending more time with her.

His Second-in-Command, Eric Gianakis, entered and plopped down in the chair facing his desk. "Got a question. I was reviewing the data on our murder investigation and happened to notice the T&R program was running."

Jay straightened. It'd only been a matter of time.

"We're monitoring Jem Wilmont. Fine. Precautionary. Great. Why haven't you mentioned it to me?"

He winced at his Second's accusing tone.

"And, while we're at it, what's with you taking her through the offices here and up in Operations? You didn't even do that when trying to impress that chef, Meizhen." Eric jabbed a finger at him. "What the hell is going on, *Chief*?"

Ouch. Eric was really pissed. Jay rubbed his neck tiredly. "The only excuse I can give is paranoia."

Eric's brows drew down. "Paranoia?" he echoed in disbelief.

Yeah, he'd been stupid. Eric Gianakis was a damn fine investigator and a friend. In the six years he'd been here, he'd dug out a number of criminals, including a couple of wannabe drug dealers. Born on a high-gravity planet, his strength had come in handy a number of times, too. He'd more than earned the Second position.

"Close the door, Eric, and I'll brief you." His friend's eyebrows reversed direction. As soon as he regained his seat, Jay began summarizing the situation. He held back his suspicion of being monitored by an internal traitor.

"She can identify him by his voice?" Eric said sharply. "She didn't get a physical look at him?" he added after Jay nodded.

Eric's fingers drummed a staccato on his thigh. "Voice alone won't stand up in court."

"I know." Jay's voice turned calculating. "But as a suspect, we can investigate, turn his life upside down."

"No telling what might shake out," Eric agreed. "But, do you know how many men are on Fulbright? The guy Miss Wilmont was damn lucky to hear at the elevator? He could have been heading up for business or personal reasons, not because he worked there."

That had occurred to Jay, belatedly. "Hate to say it, but Jem's suggestion back at the start might be our best bet."

"What was that?"

"Line all the men up and have them say a few sentences."

Eric blinked. "That would work." He paused. "If this isn't misdirection on Miss Wilmont's part."

"You mean, that she's actually the killer?" When Eric nodded, he listed the same reasons he'd given Jem. "It would have been easier for Miss Wilmont to simply say she entered, got what she needed, then exited without seeing or hearing anything. The comp system only records when staff ID is used to access an area, not how long they're there or when they leave."

"Except under surveillance."

"Except that."

"How much longer do you plan to run Track and Report?"

Jay grimaced at his friend's diplomatic question. Technically, he could activate the program short-term on any of the station's staff at his discretion—it was in the fine print. But he'd passed that legal limit several days ago. A petition to continue would probably be granted by Judge Svatora, after giving him a verbal slap and maybe a fine. Still might, if she found out.

He ran a hand across his chin and sighed. "About five minutes."

***

The server had just deposited Jem's sandwich and bowl of soup when Jay slid into the seat across from her. She gave him a lopsided smile. *Looks like I made a convert,* Jem mused, watching him select two gyros from the auto-menu. No sides, though.

"So. Any new thoughts?" she asked.

"Plenty," he said, giving her a crooked smile of his own. "Most of which go nowhere or aren't for public airing."

Jem grinned around a mouthful of lettuce, cheese, and tomato.

The Howling Monkey's dinner crowd was still trickling in, so his order arrived quickly. They ate in silence. Finished, they stacked their dishes on the table's end.

Jay glanced around, then leaned forward. "I turned off the tracking program this morning," he said in a low voice. The *Monkey's* booths didn't have sound suppression, but the rising volume of voices was a good deterrent to eavesdropping.

Jem nodded in understanding. He was telling her to be careful. "And the nosy patrollers?" she asked, giving him an impish grin.

"Nosy is part of their job description," Jay replied in a matter-of-fact tone. "*Cosmic Trails* will be making its regular stop two days from now. I've checked—there's nineteen tickets purchased, almost half of them male."

"You've not locked them out?"

"No."

Then there'd be twenty tickets after she got off work. Talk about going full circle, since that was the ship she'd arrived on.

"Instead, I'm going to vet each passenger as they board. Have them recite their name and destination." A grin flashed. "Probably get an additional line or two about having to do so from some."

And he'd expect her to be somewhere nearby, listening. Her gaze locked with his. "I promise to listen closely…and ensure I'm the last one to board."

He straightened. "You're leaving?"

"This was never meant to be a long-term stop," Jem said quietly. "I've already stayed longer than I intended. Hoping for that one-in-a-million chance to hear the killer again? Not a good reason."

"There could be other reasons for staying."

Jem pulled out her cash card, plugging it into the payment slot. Selecting *All*, she paid for his meal too. A parting gift, knowing that her silence was his answer. Flicking him a regretful smile, she managed, "Have a good day, Chief," before sliding out of the booth.

***

Jem doused water on the floor and began mopping. One more restroom and she was done for the day. Done, period. She'd turn in her resignation along with her cart. She heard the door open behind her. *Someone can't wait.*

Jem half-turned. "I'll be just a—"

A man coming toward her. *Snick.* A knife blade suddenly sticking out of his fist. Death looked out of his eyes. Her death. Everything went into slow motion as she pivoted on her heel.

He lunged. Swung.

She stepped back, twisting. Fire slashed across her side. She slammed the mop handle upwards under his jaw. Heard his teeth snap together.

He jerked back a step.

Jem shoved the mop handle into his stomach as hard as she could. Pushed.

Doubled over, he stumbled backward, slipped on the wet floor, and tumbled over the mop pail. Arms flailing, he went down. The crash of his body hitting the floor restarted time.

Panting, hands locked on her only weapon, Jem sidled past him toward the door. Blood leaking around his head halted her. *Okay, he looks out of it.* She took another step, and pain lanced across her ribs.

"Oh shit, oh shit, that hurts."

Her hand came away from her side, heavily coated in blood. *Not good.* Nor was the growing woozy feeling. The door. She needed to reach the door and then she'd call—her left leg buckled in sudden weakness, taking her down to her knees. The mop fell away. Teeth gritted, she half dragged, half pushed herself over against the wall. Panting, she glanced at her attacker. Still no movement.

Jem pulled out her phone; fumbled it when the wall lurched sideways. Then the whole room tilted, the beginning of a slow spin. Her vision was telescoping. "Stop it, stop it," she hissed. But her brain was listening about as well as it had at Myerstone. The phone blurred. Jem panicked. Hands shaking, eyes forced wide to focus better, she carefully pressed on the nine, then twice more: 9-9-9, the universal emergency number.

"Fulbright Emergency. What is the nature of your emergency?"

She tried to speak; worked to draw in breath.

"Please state the nature of your emergency."

"Stabbed. Six-D. Rest…roooom," Jem managed before everything went dark.

Chapter 18

Chief Tatarenko nodded at the officer guarding the restroom doorway and stepped inside. His gaze swept the room. Dead man on floor, blood smears on wall and floor, a blood-stained mop and, looking down, a big puddle of blood near his feet.

His gaze swung to the officer in charge. "Officer Cardoza?"

"Medics bundled Miss Wilmont upstairs. Dead guy's name is Nassar Dreyfuss," she said, handing him the man's ID and staff badge. "Employed as an elevator technician—hired seven months ago. Doubt he got this from a maintenance toolbox." She held up a bloodstained knife in an evidence baggy.

A knife that wasn't made for splicing wires or scraping grease fittings. The double-sided blade was matte black where it wasn't coated in red. The handle appeared textured, with finger grooves for a firm grip.

A tactical knife. An assassin's knife.

Tatarenko's cold gaze flicked to the dead man. "Check his locker, his quarters—anywhere he hung out and with whom; document any background info he may have mentioned." Cardoza didn't need to be told her job—she was a seasoned officer, but it gave him some sense of control. He handed back the ID and started to turn away.

"Chief? Miss Wilmont is a gutsy woman, a fighter. That's not a novice's knife and she fought him with a mop. My money says she'll pull through."

He gave her a thank-you nod, glanced at the blood puddle, and headed for Medical's Emergency section.

Thirty long minutes later, a doctor came striding into the waiting room. Jay surged to his feet, relief and worry mixed. Doctor James Brodersen was the Senior Medical lead, one step down from the Chief Medical Director.

"I assume you're here about Miss Wilmont," Brodersen said, unsmiling. "She has a ten-centimeter wound between the fifth and sixth ribs and was suffering from Hypovolemic shock and ARDS when she arrived."

Tatarenko gave him a blank look.

"Severe blood lost and respiratory distress," he clarified. "She's on a ventilator and we began a transfusion as soon as the wound was closed. Blood pressure should stabilize after her blood and fluid levels are brought up."

"Complications?"

"None expected at this point, Chief, as Miss Wilmont arrived fairly quickly after receiving the injury. She will be closely monitored in ICU to ensure that. Barring anything unexpected, I anticipate a full recovery."

Relief washed over him. "I'll be stationing guards outside—"

"Dr. Brodersen to ICU, Code Blue. Dr. Brodersen to ICU. Code Blue."

The doctor bolted out of the waiting room before the intercom finished its message.

"How many patients in ICU?" Tatarenko asked the somber nurse-receptionist.

"One."

Jay stalked out into the corridor, resisting the urge to punch a wall. He took a deep breath, then let it out slowly as he worked to calm his churning emotions. Somewhat successful, he pulled out his phone and called his Second.

"What do we have on Nassar Dreyfuss?" he snapped.

"Not a lot. We've got his locker and room contents inventoried; nothing outstanding there. All his phone contacts, call or text, are wiped. He worked on the midnight crew; Officer Cardoza is still interviewing his coworkers. I've got a priority message filed with UPMS for Delmark Three's Federal Law Enforcement—that's listed as his home planet."

It'd be at least a week before they got a response. Stuck out here in Taurus's heliosphere, Fulbright's mail pods only went between them and Aldebaran, Taurus Two. Everything outbound would be sorted by the main UPMS facility there and then sent on to their designated destinations. The pod would return with the station's mail and messages.

"Send a polite request to Aldebaran's Planetary Defense Office. Commander Whoever can go through military channels to find if-what-where military service he may have had."

"Will do." Pause. *"Miss Wilmont?"*

His pulse skipped a beat. "I'll let you know." He disconnected and went back into the waiting room.

***

"Not your usual style," Eric said, sliding into the booth.

Surly, Jay said, "It's growing on me." He'd called his Second to meet him in *The Howling Monkey*. Eric's eyes flicked to the beer his hand curled around, but didn't say anything. Screw it. "Update me," Jay said, taking his first sip.

Basically nothing, he fumed, as Eric listed what little they'd found physically or by interview. But when Eric said Dreyfuss probably was ex-military, he straightened.

"One interviewee," Eric continued, "himself ex-army, is pretty sure of it. Said it wasn't anything specific, much less actually said since our dead guy didn't talk about himself. It was a lot of little things that added

126

up for him."

Yeah, those small tells would catch you every time.

"Then there's that knife of his," Eric said. "The lab says it's a Mackintosh Tanto OTF—meaning the blade is released straight out the front. Deadly as hell and very popular with army ground troops."

"Did you get the message off to the PDO?" He frowned when Eric shook his head.

"After getting *that* report, I contacted the PD Office directly, explained the situation and got put through to the Commander. Figured that'd save time and, just so you know, it's General Elizabeth Chen." Amusement lit his face. "I dare you to call that woman General 'Whoever.' She had me sitting straight over a comm link."

Jay snorted out a laugh.

"Anyway, she'll provide us with whatever she finds as long as it's not classified. What about Miss Wilmont? All the nurse would tell me was that she's stable."

Jay took a swallow of beer. "She developed AHTR, medical lingo for an acute hemo-something, which translates to an adverse reaction to the blood transfusion. Fortunately, it was caught early by an exceptionally sharp-eyed young intern monitoring the process. Dammit, I shouldn't have terminated the T&R."

"This is not on you," Eric replied brusquely. "Tracking her wouldn't have prevented this, only shown us where to find the body."

Jay flinched. Flinched again when his phone went off. The ID listed it as Marv Gustav, Fulbright Station Manager.

"Yes, Mr. Gustav," he said into it. Eric made a face and leaned back.

"There's a shuttle arriving from Aldebaran at 2230, approximately, bringing a very expensive cooler of blood. A medic will sign for it, but I want you, specifically, to provide escort for it. Considering that you haven't broken that theft ring yet, I don't want the medic waylaid and it

disappearing into the black market."

"Understood," Jay said, grimacing. That was a double slap.

"*Speaking of escort, the next time you want to show off, please alert my office ahead of time so that someone who isn't busy can provide it. Gustav out.*"

Jay looked across the table. His friend was staring at the ceiling, lips pressed together. "Don't choke on it," he growled. "Go ahead, let it out."

Eric merely chuckled. "Guess that's his way of payback. Is it really that expensive?"

"My request to have two additional officers appended to this year's budget will be dropping to just one. And that's for only six units of blood, plus transport," he added as Eric's mouth dropped open. "Ever heard of Rh-null? Me neither. It's so rare, the Chukta Medical Institute, the largest medical facility on Aldebaran, has—had only thirty-one units. According to Dr. Brodersen, we were lucky they had what we needed. Evidently, it's that scarce Republic-wide."

"Incredible. Rh-null people must have bodyguards to keep from being drained dry. Miss Wilmont has that?"

"No. She has an unknown antigen in her blood, which means that at least one of her parents wasn't Earth born. Due to the severe blood loss, they'd just done a quick type-match to B-positive to get the transfusion started. The antibodies in her blood, what she has remaining, attacked what they were giving her. When she began having trouble breathing, they stopped it and analyzed further." He'd had a bit of trouble himself when the doctor told him that. "Rh-null has no antigens, making it a universal donor…critical in Jem's case."

"Incredible," Eric repeated. He glanced at the digital chronometer on the wall. "Okay, we got several hours, so I might as well have a beer while we wait."

"We?" Jay said, watching him make a selection on the auto-menu.

"If it's that damn pricy, those thieves might risk jumping you. Both of us? Uh-uh."

"If they did," Jay drawled, "we'd be able to identify them and break the ring up."

"Not worth it," Eric said. It only took a minute for a server to set a frosty glass of dark amber liquid in front of him." He held up his glass.

Jay clinked his against it and they both took a large swig.

***

They and the medic met the shuttle in the docking bay. They all had to show ID, verified by Operations, before the burly pilot would allow them on board. The Chukta's medic got their medic's signature and off they went to Medical. Nothing exciting happened on the way. Dr. Brodersen himself met them at the receptionist desk.

"How's Miss Wilmont?" Jay couldn't help asking.

"Holding her own," Brodersen replied. "We've been giving her fluids, antibiotics, and blood thinners to counteract the AHTR and stave off additional problems. This," he nodded toward the hallway the medic had vanished down, "should fix up her, assuming there aren't any other underlying issues or surprises. I ordered the extra units just in case. She'll be monitored closely, and we'll do a full scan once her status improves. If there's any damage to her organs, I expect it to be minimal."

"How long for recovery?" Eric asked.

"That depends," the doctor replied. "Most of it on Miss Wilmont. Transfusion recovery is normally only a few days. The knife wound is longer, naturally, plus the trauma from it may slow down her system's normal healing cycle. I'd like to keep her here for one to two weeks, long enough to ensure the wound is well on its way to healing and there are no lingering repercussions from her adverse reaction to the transfusion. Really. Miss Wilmont's red blood cells are quite unique. I wonder if she would consent to providing a sample once she's recuperated."

The nurse-receptionist behind him rolled her eyes.

"She should be conscious by tomorrow evening, Chief Tatarenko, if you need to interview her."

Yes, he did. They thanked the doctor and walked out.

"Now what?" Eric asked.

It was going on midnight. "Bed. Then tomorrow," Jay's voice hardened, "we start digging."

Chapter 19

The Chief went slowly, line by line, through Officer Cardoza's report. As expected, she'd thoroughly covered all aspects in her interviews, documented their responses, then provided a summary and personal conclusion at the end. The list of Nassar Dreyfuss's personal items was underwhelming. He would have passed as unremarkable, if it weren't for the events of yesterday and the bloody knife in evidence.

Then he did the same with the reports on Pauline Christiansen's file. Same results. No clues, nothing to identify the mastermind.

He was massaging the bridge of his nose when Eric sauntered in.

"Want to have an early lunch?" his Second asked.

"Where've you been?" he said, a little bit crossly.

Eric's head tilted. "Out trying to track those thieves. They hit Claybourn's Electronics in Four-C last night."

Jay let out an exasperated breath. "Sorry. I've spent the morning reviewing all the reports and information on our two hot cases. Trying to hunt down anything that might conceivably pass as leads."

"It seems to me, Miss Wilmont solved both. Christiansen's killer tracked her down, attacked with intent to kill, but ended up dead himself. Both cases closed."

"Jem's attacker was not Christiansen's killer."

His Second stiffened. "Are you sure? How do you know?"

"I doubt Dreyfuss's knife was ever far from him; why didn't he use it on Christiansen?" Jay asked, an eyebrow cocked.

"Different method, different person," Eric said, blowing out a loud breath.

"Uh-huh. My take? Christiansen retrieved the drugs from however they came in, then refused to turn them over until she got a bigger paycheck. The drug kingpin met with her, lost his temper when she wouldn't back down, grabbed something and killed her. Which is why it had to be the top dog—a lesser wouldn't have dared without getting the drugs first or we'd have another body somewhere."

Eric nodded. "Makes sense."

"Then he stuffed her into the closet, thinking he was in the clear since he'd followed her in on her staff access. Probably intended to have his gang—number unknown—start doing discreet searches. Then, lo and behold, we find the drugs in her quarters. I'm sure that burned his ass."

"Undoubtedly, if he knew about it. We kept it quiet per your orders."

"Oh, he knew. The same way he learned about Jem." Hands in his lap, Jay leaned forward. "The bastard is in our system, watching every damn thing we do. He saw the report on Jem Wilmont and realized she could recognize his voice. After he saw we were tracking her movements, I'm willing to bet he saw through our tours—figured out what we were doing. When he saw the T&R was discontinued, he used it himself to find Jem's location and sent his killer minion after her. And," Jay added, settling back in his seat, "he used your credentials and password to access it from a public comp on Six-C."

Eric practically fell into the chair in front of Jay's desk. "Mine?" A too-quick-to-decipher expression flashed across his face. "The audit file."

Jay shook his head. "Deleted. Again, using your account privileges."

Petros Hu, his network administrator, had come screeching into his office mid-morning, informing him yesterday's audit file had been tampered with. *"There's nothing prior to 1512, sir."*

Eric's eyebrows jumped up to his hairline. "Then how?"

Jay's smile was full of teeth. "I set up a monitoring program of my own running parallel to the audit." A precaution after realizing they were being watched. He had immediately checked his copy. Intact, it revealed his Second's information was used to reactivate T&R at 1448. Checking Wilmont's file, he found its last updated entry was 1509: twelve minutes before her call to Emergency.

Jay continued as Eric's eyes widened. "The SOB activated T&R during the time you were helping to stop that big fight in Seven-D's lounge. After the bastard watched long enough to ensure her position didn't change, he terminated it and then deleted the audit file to hide his actions. Being a pro, Dreyfuss wiped his phone before engaging his target in case he's captured or killed. Which did happen this time. By the way, if you'd tried to log into the system in the last two hours, you'd have found your account locked."

"Well, shit." Eric ran a hand through his hair. "I'll change my password."

"Eventually. For now, it stays locked."

"How the hell do you expect me to work?" Eric said stiffly.

"The others can log you in as needed under their credentials. In the meantime, continue working on that theft ring. We really need—"

"You don't trust me," he said flatly.

"I don't trust the frigging bastard who's in our system," Jay snapped. "No telling what he's put in the network using your credentials."

"The account was compromised, not me. Changing my password—"

"No. I won't risk it."

Eric's jaw flexed. He pushed out of the chair hard enough that one of the arms snapped off the back. "If you'll excuse me, Chief, I need to find a babysitter so I can check my messages."

"This is temporary, Eric."

"Right!" he flung over his shoulder.

Jay stared thoughtfully at the broken chair and empty doorway.

Chapter 20

Propped up in bed, Jem smiled weakly at the Chief when he peeked hesitantly in the door. "I'm awake. And mostly decent," she said in an attempt at humor. When they'd rolled her out of ICU a couple of hours ago, she'd insisted on something larger than what was barely covering her.

He returned her smile as he entered. "Yeah, hospital gowns can be revealing." His gaze roamed over her.

Jem knew what he saw. Pale skin, wires attached to a half-exposed breast, an IV draining into an arm. At least her hair was braided, courtesy of a nurse. "I know, I look terrible."

"You look better than I expected. How do you feel?"

"Like a kitten could bat me wall-to-wall without a lick of effort," she said on a sigh. He grinned. "But at least I'm here," she added, plucking at the blanket covering her. "I'm told the other guy didn't make it." She'd killed him.

"I didn't mean to," gushed out before she could stop it. "Honestly. I-I just wanted to push him away to get to the door I didn't mean to shove so hard I didn't mean to to—" She stumbled to a halt when he reached over the side rail and laid his hand on the one clenching the blanket. Moisture pricked her eyes.

"Justified defense, Jem," he said gently but firmly. "Nassar Dreyfuss attacked with a knife. You defended yourself. With adrenaline and a *mop*, no less. Legal has officially ruled it as such. I got the email about an hour ago."

"That quick?" she asked, blinking back the tears.

An eyebrow quirked. "Evidence was pretty straightforward."

The door opened, admitting a nurse with a tray of food. Jay stepped back so he could push the rollable table into position.

"Got a good, hearty supper for you, Miss Wilmont. Your system might be topped off, but your body still has a lot of repairing to do," he said cheerily. "Name's Wilson, I'll be at your beck and call tonight. Just push the button," he said, indicating the control beside her. "Make sure she eats it all, Chief." With a wave of his hand, he was gone.

They both stared at the door for a moment.

"Well," Jem said, "it's nice to know the person looking after you enjoys his job. You've got a lot going on, Chief, there's no need to stay," she said, feeling a bit awkward.

"Yes, I have things to do. Several of which is speaking with you. And it's Jay." His gaze was steady. "I consider us friends, even if there's nothing more. Now, you eat while I talk." He pulled up the visitor's chair.

The meal was good, the conversation was productive.

Jay summarized what they'd learned so far about Dreyfuss. Jem described the events in the restroom and admitted to getting lucky. "I'm not a fighter—not physically," she added. "I've had a mostly bland life." Until recently. A collage of smiling, laughing faces swirled before her mind's eye: Dani, Christine, Marion, Ned, Janet, Mr. Petrov. Then Myerstone's blackened shell shoved itself forward. She wrenched herself away from the memories to see Jay's too-perceptive gaze.

Jem managed another smile, a wry one this time. "Guess I better learn. Might not be so lucky next time." She'd damn well better learn to fight here, on the physical plane. It hadn't occurred to her, not even once, to use her ability during the attack. The guy—*Dreyfuss, his name was Nassar Dreyfuss*—would be alive if she'd protected herself by *shifting* away.

Only… Jem stabbed at her baked potato remnant. What fallout would she have had to live with afterward? Did it matter? She already had one stalker. Sooner or later, she'll have to deal with others knowing about her. Unless she completely hermitized herself, there was no way she could go her whole life without this, this curse becoming known. *Shift* or not *shift*? How often would she have to ask herself that, and how often would it require a split-second decision? She was so not ready for this.

"You expect another time?" Jay asked, breaking the silence with a neutral tone.

"Life is full of unexpected turns. I have no idea what the Universe is going to throw my way next." Wasn't that the frigging truth. Which also had his arms crossing and his brain a twirling. Oops. "What else did you want to talk about?"

His right fingers drummed a fast staccato on his left forearm. Oh yeah, he knew she was deflecting. Thankfully, he decided to let it pass.

"About vetting the passengers as they board the shuttle tomorrow," Jay finally said.

Jem found herself nodding as he outlined his plan. It was a good one. Simple, but effective, and didn't take long to go over the details. A good thing, too, because her brain was wanting to shut down.

Silence fell. So did her eyelids. Jem managed to pull them back open when she felt the kiss on her forehead.

"Get some sleep," he told her. "We'll coordinate in the morning."

She was asleep before he was out the door.

***

Mid-morning found Jem listening closely to a portable table comp with Officer Roy Zimmerman. He'd rolled it up to her bed a half hour ago. The young officer was officially here as her protection detail, but had been fully briefed on their plan and the necessity of keeping the particulars secret. A plan now in motion as the Star Liner *Cosmic Trail* hung a half kilometer off the station's side, waiting for its passengers.

At Jay's signal, they'd linked to the shuttle bay's computer, engaging their comp's video mode but muting its audio. Jay had done the reverse, activating the audio on his comp while keeping the video blocked. This allowed her and Officer Zimmerman to see and hear the shuttle bay's activities while keeping them hidden.

"Morning, folks. For those who don't know, I'm Security Chief Jay Tatarenko. I know you're ready and anxious to get underway so I'll make this quick. We're testing a new voice identification system."

Zimmerman gave her a lopsided grin. "Can't get him for lying."

Jay explained what he wanted them to do. With only a few grumbles, each one recited their name and destination into the computer before boarding the transfer shuttle. Even the women were asked to make a recording, hiding both the true nature of the 'VI system' and who they were looking for.

As the last person boarded and the shuttle door closed, Jem shook her head at Zimmerman. Their killer hadn't been one of them. Jay moved in front of the comp and activated video on his end.

"Everything go okay?" he asked, keeping it vague for listening ears.

"Yes, sir," Zimmerman replied, after unmuting their audio. "All responses were clear, and none produced negative flags."

"On my way." The screen blanked.

Zimmerman pushed the comp off to the side and they chatted. Jem managed to keep it mostly about him, his goals, and the vacation on Aldebaran he'd recently returned from. He was right proud to be a Taurus System native. He stood when Jay came through the door.

"Chief."

"Officer Zimmerman." Jay acknowledged. "You did well. You may resume your post now."

"Sir. Ma'am." The young man strode from the room.

Jem knew he'd be standing outside her hospital room. "He's a nice guy. Sharp. Sees himself in your chair in the future," she said, grinning.

"Given his performance since he signed on several years ago, and what I personally know of him, he'd make it proud. How are you?"

"Weak. I feel a nap coming on."

"Not surprised. Rest is best. After you get a bit stronger, we'll talk. I might have a way to flush Pauline Christiansen's killer out."

Jem set straight up. "How?"

He shook his head. "Still working on it."

"Not even a hint? Spoilsport." Jem crossed her arms and pretended to pout.

Jay laughed. "Consider it an incentive toward healing."

The man actually had the audacity to pat her on the head before leaving.

Chapter 21

Chief Tatarenko watched his Second stalk into his office and sit, ramrod straight and unsmiling, in the seat directly opposite him. "Eric."

"Chief."

The tension between them had filtered all the way down to the newest Security recruit. The reasons of what and why hadn't filtered—they'd practically detonated. Eric's attitude for the past six days certainly hadn't helped, and had, in fact, alienated a number of people, including several of the senior officers. There'd almost been a brawl in the break room yesterday between Eric Gianakis and Senior Officer Hannah Jones when she accused him of "inappropriate and unreasonable attitude for the only reasonable action given the circumstances." Two others had put limbs in danger by stepping between them.

To say his Second had become a disappointment was an understatement. Especially the snappish, snarly personality change. He wouldn't be surprised if there were bets going around whether or not he appointed a new Second-in-Command.

Both voice and features noncommittal, Jay said, "You'll have access to the network by lunch time. Petros Hu is building you a new profile as we speak. He'll call you in when it's ready."

Eric's shoulders only relaxed partway. "A new profile?"

"Network security has finished scrubbing the system. They found two unknown and questionable programs: one residing in memory, the other in the communications server. They've been deleted as has your old profile. Online sniffers will be watching in case they missed something."

Eric's body language changed. "Excellent," he said, his tone jovial. "No need to keep bothering the others now."

Bothering? "Antagonistic" was what he'd overheard two young officers describe it, along with a few non-complementary addendums. When he didn't respond in kind, Eric's smile dimmed and a wary look entered his eyes. Jay let the silence sit for several seconds, then, "Cargo/transport *Clovis Two* is scheduled three days from now. There's several on the waiting list for passage out. I want you to do the voice ID check on the passengers like I did for the *Cosmic Trail*. Jem will be listening from her quarters."

"Her quarters?" Eric said neutrally.

"She's undergoing tests. With no issues, she'll be released from Medical this afternoon. Dr. Brodersen will clear her for light duty in another week if she continues to progress well. The patrol schedule is being revised to include sweeps through her residential corridor. In the meantime, she'll be reviewing voice entries. I'm ordering all Security personnel to provide a two or three sentence recording to our admin office. If Jem determines all are negative, I'll request the same from Operations and then down through all departments as needed. You'll continue to handle those departing through commercial or private means. I want this guy found."

Eric stirred. "Wouldn't it make more sense for one of the junior officers to do the checks? It's supposedly only in testing."

"My presence made it a high-interest item. My orders stand."

Eric's face blanked. "Orders. Understood, Chief Tatarenko. May I go?"

"Dismissed."

Jay watched his ex-friend's stiff exit. *At least he didn't break the chair this time*. He didn't miss the sideways look of several young officers casually passing his doorway. Yep, there were bets.

He passed the rest of morning reviewing files and double-checking his data. The facts still came to the same conclusion. Now he just needed Jem to confirm it. The call from Medical came shortly after noon. She was being released.

Jay stood as Jem was wheeled into the waiting room. She flashed him a smile as Dr. Brodersen strode up behind her.

"Medic O'Brian will see Miss Wilmont to her quarters. Now, Miss Wilmont," Dr. Brodersen said sternly, "you've agreed to call if there are any aches, pains, or changes of any nature. I find out different, you'll be back here."

Jem made a face. "Yes, sir."

"Chief? I can count on you to mediate her behavior?"

"I can promise to try," Jay said dryly.

Brodersen scowled as both Jem and the medic snickered.

With a final wave good-by, the three of them headed for the nearest elevator. Elevator reached, L-7 button pressed, doors closed. As they started downward, Jem looked up at the medic.

"No offense, Mr. O'Brian, but I'm glad to be out of there."

He grinned down at her and winked. "No offense, Miss Wilmont, but we are too."

It was Jay's turn to snicker.

Jem switched to a comfy chair when they reached her quarters. With a final admonishment about taking it easy and to avoid any twisting or sudden movements, O'Brian wheeled the empty chair out.

"Can I get you anything?" Jay asked.

"No, thank you." Pause. "Is tonight on?"

"Yes."

Jem's eyes searched his face. "Proving one of your own is a killer has to be hard."

More than hard. "All the more reason he has to be stopped. I've sprinkled the crumbs. If he follows them," Jay shrugged, "what happens, happens."

* * * * *

Click.

The soft sound warned Jem that her door was being opened. Jem *shifted* as the corridor's soft lighting appeared in a narrow slit. *Checking? Thinking the darkened room means I'm in bed? Surprise!* After a couple of seconds, the door opened fully and light fell partially across the corner chair where she sat, invisible. A silhouette quickly slipped in, closing the door and returning the room to darkness.

Wouldn't do for someone to come along and spot you.

Technically, the room was just mostly dark. Pale green lights strategically located along the floor/wall seams kept the number of tripping accidents and medical visits to a minimum. Jem watched the shape slowly make its way across the room. When it reached the bedroom door, Jem *shifted* back and turned on the lamp beside her.

Eric Gianakis whirled around. He blinked rapidly at the additional light.

"You make a habit of creeping into people's quarters in the middle of the night?"

"I was checking to make sure you were doing okay. Didn't want the Chief to worry."

She cocked her head. "Yeah, that was your voice I heard in Supply Two. You're the station's drug kingpin. You killed Miss Christiansen. You sent Dreyfuss to kill me, only he failed."

He let out a deep sigh. "A first—and last—for him," he said, pulling a syringe from his jacket pocket. "I'll have to finish it."

He took several steps toward her, halting when Jem pulled a stunner out from beside her.

"I knew you'd try again. That's why I'm sitting here." Jem's smile was cold. "I've been waiting for you."

"Really?"

"Uh-huh. You've been smart, but overconfidence finally tripped you up."

"Really?" he repeated, sounding amused.

"You supposedly headed to Seven-D to assist in quelling a lounge brawl. Instead, you got off the elevator on Six and went to a public comp in Section-C." Not so amused now. "You accessed the tracking program to get my location and then contacted Nassar Dreyfuss. After deleting the audit file to cover your tracks, you took the stairwell down to Level Seven and proceeded to 'assist' the officers."

Gianakis glowered at her. "How the hell do you know that?"

She shrugged. "Jay told me."

Gianakis looked momentarily stunned. "How did *he* know?"

"He figured it out after you did something to trip his inner warning bell. He started digging, asking questions, and found things that didn't line up. Like the short-notice delay of Shaymus Stanton's interview that you still logged as held at the scheduled time, which coincided with the timeframe of Miss Christiansen's killing. Or that lounge ruckus you supposedly helped quell? The officers that actually did the work said you didn't show up until it was pretty much contained. Then came your biggest oops.

"When you deleted the day's audit file, it automatically created a new one at the next recorded activity. Want to guess what that was?" Jem waited a beat. "Your badge accessing the stairwell in Six-C that's, coincidentally, right next to the public comp that was used." She waited another beat. "When you supposedly took the elevator straight down to Level Seven."

His lips pursed. "Damn. I'll have to remember that in the future."

"You don't have a future. At least, not here."

"That's true. It appears I'm going to have to shut down operations here. As for the rest? Chief Tatarenko can be suspicious all he wants, but it's all circumstantial and coincidence. All he has, officially, is misconduct and maybe dereliction of duty that will warrant my dismissal. I'll save him the trouble and resign. He can't prove anything else…not without you and those damn ears of yours."

He raised the syringe. Jem raised the stunner.

He smirked. Jem frowned.

Wary, she said, "Jay's order for voice samples was to force your hand. You couldn't allow me to hear it and you couldn't afford to refuse providing one. We knew you'd have to come yourself, using your master key to override my door's security."

"Which I have. Twice now."

Jem's brows drew down. Twice?

"The Chief shouldn't have left you here alone." Gianakis's smirk was pure malice. "Audits don't include access to private quarters. If that stunner is the one from your bedside drawer, I rendered it non-functional earlier. I paid a visit when he took you to dinner. Figured you might have weaponed up."

She pulled the trigger; nothing happened. *Good thing Plan B was in place.*

His smirk widened. "I also checked to make sure the Chief didn't stay for after dinner activities. He's in his quarters and no, it can't be traced back to me."

"I see. One of your babysitters wasn't careful enough when logging you in. Did you bother deleting the audit file, again, after using their credentials to access T&R? Doesn't matter. We figured you might check on one or both of us, so we went the old-fashioned way," Jem said nonchalantly, keeping her gaze off the bedroom door opening silently behind him.

"Old-fashioned?" he said, cautiously.

"*Human* surveillance and someone you wouldn't think to check on."

"Which works two-fold as a witness," Senior Officer Jones said, stepping out of the bedroom.

Gianakis spun on his heel as Officer Zimmerman slipped out and took a position to her left. Both were pointing stunners at him.

"Chief Tatarenko?" Jem asked.

"On his way. I sent a text as soon as I heard your voices. Drop the syringe."

Rather than dropping it, Gianakis gave a negligent toss. When three pairs of eyes instinctively glanced at it, he *moved*. One second he was in the middle of the room, the next his hand was wrapped tightly around Jem's throat and yanking her up in front of him. Since they were about the same height, her body fully shielded his.

High-grav speed at its finest, was Jem's errant thought.

"Shoot, and I'll break her neck before I go down," Gianakis warned over her shoulder.

Chapter 22

Click.

The Chief entered, using his own master key. Jay's eyes went to Jem's.

"Small hitch in our plans," she managed to croak out.

Jay studied the man for a moment. "Why?" he quietly asked. "You had a good future, people respected you. I respected, trusted you."

"A good future?" Eric snorted. "Forty, fifty years of putting up with stupid, snobby people for a measly pension? I was going to retire in ten years. *Ten years*," he all but shouted. "Then she has to ruin it," he said, his fingers tightening.

Jem gasped at the constriction, then coughed as his hand relaxed.

Jay took a step forward. "Let her go, Eric. Don't do anything to make this worse."

"Worse?" He gave a hollow laugh. "Drugs. Murder. I'm already earmarked for Hellspawn."

It was a barren, sweltering planet with more lava pools than solid ground. It was a Federal Penitentiary planet, the final home for those with life sentences.

"What you are going to do, *Chief*," Eric continued, "is have the Operations Manager prep that Class One of his. I'll need a pilot and food for three. When we get to where I tell him, I'll let both go and fade away."

Jay saw Jem's painful grimace as Eric's hand flexed. His hand clenched. "Let. Her. Go," he said, glaring at his ex-Second.

"Nope. I've got nothing to lose, but you do. You going to call Gustav, or watch me twist her head off?" He leered at Tatarenko. "Don't know my own strength sometimes. I hit poor Pauline a bit harder than I meant to."

Knuckles. That was the odd indents in her skull the experts couldn't figure out. Glancing at Jem, he saw her eyebrows bob several times. She repeated it at Officer Jones. *She was planning something.*

"Well?" Eric demanded.

Jay pulled his phone out slowly, hoping that whatever Jem was about to do, wouldn't get her killed. He nearly cursed when her hand rolled into a fist. *He's high-grav. Punching him won't do—*

Jem's fist slammed backward into Eric's balls.

—except that. Jay couldn't hold back a sympathetic wince.

Eric grunted, his body tilting sideways. His grip must have loosened because Jem jerked and then dropped straight down. Officers Jones and Zimmerman fired. Eric's body tilted all the way sideways and he crashed to the floor.

Jay rushed over and helped Jem stand.

"Figured he wouldn't expect that. *Owww*," she moaned, holding her side. He lowered her back into the chair.

"Officer Jones, handcuff the prisoner. Officer Zimmerman call Medical, inform them we need a medic. That was a damn risky move, Jem. If his hand had spasmed, he'd have crushed your throat."

Jem merely gave him a weak grin.

The response was swift, with Dr. Brodersen himself following the medic into Jem's quarters. Once their surprise was over, he had the medic call for a grav-gurney to take Gianakis to Medical. A double-stun shot probably hadn't hurt his high gravity physique, but the doctor still insisted he be evaluated. Jones and Zimmerman accompanied him as guards.

"No, I'm not going to Medical," Jem told Brodersen firmly. "It's not bleeding so I didn't break it open. I'm just…sore."

"You may have pulled a muscle."

"Well, then, Doc," she drawled, "it's not going to heal any faster up there than it is down here."

Brodersen scowled, looked over at the Chief.

Jay's upward turned palm said, 'leave me out of this.'

"Fine. I still want to examine your side."

Jem stood, winced, then led the doctor into the bedroom. Ten minutes later, they returned.

"Chief, I'll send word on Gianakis's condition." Dr. Brodersen said. Giving them both a curt nod, he left with an ill-tempered stomp.

"He really wants to get you back into Medical," Jay said.

* * * * *

"What he wants is a case study." Jem sighed, and settled gently back into her chair. It was just the two of them now.

"Your blood?"

"Uh-huh. Told him I needed to keep what I had. Nor do I feel like being prodded and poked, even in the name of science." Especially if he did a DNA analysis. "I pointed him to Venice Two. That's actually where I was born, me and my father. We moved to Earth, my mother's birthplace, when I was two, which is why I consider myself an Earther. I'm sorry about your friend."

Jay shook his head. "I don't understand. He could have taken another position somewhere else, even gone private, if money was that important to him."

Jem had no answer as an uneasy silence stretched between them.

He stuck his hands in his pockets; looked at her. "What now?" he asked quietly.

She knew what he was asking. Just as quietly, she said, "Rest. Heal. See if the *Clovis* has room for another passenger."

His lips pressed together and his chin dipped once in acknowledgement. "Then I'll let you get started. Thank you for your help in closing this case."

Jem stared at the door long minutes after he left. No, she couldn't stay. How long before Reginald Kurzvall or his thugs found her? Who would they hurt to get her? The only way to prevent that, to protect others, was to keep moving. To keep to herself.

For the first time she saw, she truly understood, the loneliness that lay ahead. Felt the first tendrils of it wrapping around her soul. Felt the first tear slide down her cheek.

Chapter 23

Zorinsky Science Station, Mandoria Habitat, Malver II, Wolf I, Hanmark IV. Jem read the destination list the *Clovis* had posted as it approached Fulbright, along with notice of five available passenger berths. She clicked on the link for Malver, the first planetary stop. Well, crap. Subterranean cities due to a highly toxic and irradiated surface? Big nope.

Wolf One was an agriculture planet with widely spaced cities between vast farms. It was also over three weeks transit from Fulbright. Longer than she wanted, which ruled out even more distant Hanmark.

Jem chewed on her lip. The science station would have little in the way of job opportunities and she was kind of tired of scrubbing toilets. She clicked on Mandoria Habitat and scanned the accompanying info. It was an eight-day transit and its primary purpose was support for the Ellison Mining Company, which owned the mining rights to the planet it orbited. Miners equaled bars, probably a lot of them in this case. While she'd really prefer to be planet-side again, it was doable. The habitat should also be a step up from this station and pay better.

Departure was…TBD. What?

Jem hurriedly purchased a ticket, then contacted the employment office. Miss Henderson was a bit miffed at her no-notice termination, despite the fact she hadn't been working since her attack. When Jem inquired about a refund from Facilities Management for the remaining week's rent, that woman looked down her nose and disconnected the video call. *That's a no.*

Jem finished packing and headed for the Finance Office. There she withdrew her remaining credits and closed her employee account. Then she hurried toward the shuttle terminal, not caring how long she had to wait. She wasn't missing her ride. Everything she'd needed to do here was done.

She'd documented and signed a formal report of the events in her quarters. Dr. Brodersen, slightly miffed she wasn't leaving a sample behind, had given her a final exam and had deemed the wound healed enough to fully release her. Jay had taken her to *Meizhen's* last night for a farewell dinner. He'd told her there were only two other names on the waiting list and he'd never seen the *Clovis* arrive with fewer than four available berths. The evening hadn't been awkward, as both of them had fallen into the 'just friends' vibe over the last few days. Still, Jem saw the sad resignation in his eyes when they said their good-byes.

Two hours and forty-two minutes later, Jem watched the Fulbright Station receding on the *Clovis's* lounge viewscreen. *Have a good, normal life, Jay.*

Chapter 24

Mandoria, the Klaxton System's only planet, was rich in rare and heavy metals. It was also a toxic, 5-Eg gravitation nightmare with unpredictable storms. Everyone lived on the habitat that orbited above it. Jem studied her new temporary home on the lounge viewscreen as the *Clovis II* eased up to the long docking arm on this end of it, which was pointed away from the planet. She'd reviewed what info the ship's database had on it several times during their eight-day transit. The data said the huge construct was 100 meters tall, a kilometer long, 300 meters wide, and up to twenty levels, depending on the section.

Seeing it up close, it looked a whole lot bigger.

There would be another docking arm on the habitat's other end, but on the opposite side and pointing toward the planet. That one was dedicated to all things mining, as was that whole end of the habitat. She'd barely skimmed the info on the Ellison Mining Company, as she had no interest in it. Instead, she'd read the sections listing available services and amenities. From the number listed, she shouldn't have trouble finding a job.

The viewscreen blanked and the ship's intercom clicked on.

"We're in geostationary synch with the Mandoria Habitat," the captain said. "All passengers prepare to disembark. Loadmaster, disengage rear grav-field and open cargo doors." The intercom clicked off.

Well, that was rather terse. Jem glanced at her fellow passengers. The three also getting off here were already heading for the plazo below, bags in hand. Well, the two taking the lift down did. The one practically sliding down the stairwell rungs had his slung over his shoulder. *What's their hurry? Can't go anywhere until the access tube is attached to the ship's hatch.*

And there it was, from the sound of it. Sighing, Jem gathered her two bags and stood. Not about to attempt the stairwell, she pressed the return switch for the lift. By the time it deposited her below, the hatch was open and the three men gone. An older, grizzled crewman stood next to it. Addams, that was his name. She'd enjoyed a couple of chess games with him on the way here. A nice guy, although he hid it behind a gruff demeanor.

"You sure you want to get off here?" his gravelly voice asked as Jem approached.

Jem blinked in surprise. Ah. He was thinking of the problems she might run into. From what she'd read, the mining below was pretty difficult. Work that couldn't be automated had to be done in specially adapted equipment. Only the hardest, toughest, and undoubtedly the meanest miners would last long here.

She gave Addams a wry smile. "Thank you, but I'll be okay."

He gave a noncommittal grunt, then motioned her forward. He correctly interpreted Jem's hesitation at the tube's entrance. "No low-G experience? There's grav-nodules between the ribs. They're set to half-G, so no bouncing," he warned.

Jem flashed him a grateful smile. Hefting one bag on her shoulder, she started down the tube. The hatch clanged shut behind her. Odd, that almost sounded…ominous. At a half-G, it was hard not to bounce down the ten-meter tube. She stepped out into a fairly barren reception room. It held a row of chairs and two large, battered-looking men in security uniforms leaning against the wall. Their conversation halted mid-sentence, their stares sending a prickle down her spine.

Jem gave a cautious nod as she walked past them and on down the long corridor. Guess security would need to be as tough as the ones they're meant to control. The motion-sensitive door at the end opened and she was in the habitat proper. She paused at the elevator doors just inside and read the large sign displayed prominently next to them. It said all new arrivals were to check in with the Habitat Administrative Office on Level C-3, suite 3101.

Well, that made things easy. She pressed the call button.

Reaching this section's third level, she stepped out into a small, mostly coverall-wearing crowd and what the ship's data had called a node. Nodes were recessed waiting areas for either an elevator or a slider, elevators that traveled horizontally between the Sections. Handy, considering this monstrosity's length. Not to mention, the Habitat Administration offices were located almost in the middle of the frigging thing.

Waiting with the others, Jem glanced down the well-lit, wide corridor that opened off the node. Nice, even on this end of the habitat. Section E according to the info, was dedicated to warehouses, storage, all things maintenance, and facility odds-and-ends, like the habitat's docking arm and cargo bays. It even had a small crematorium tucked in a back corner. Offices and workshops were in the majority here.

A half hour later, Jem threw herself down on a comfy bed. Her room on D-12 was not only larger than expected, it was outfitted better than some places she'd stayed on Earth. It had a mid-sized viewscreen on the wall as well as a table comp. The bathroom even had an honest-to-goodness tub with shower. All perks to entice people to stay, she figured. Wishing she could roll over and go to sleep, Jem reluctantly pushed herself up instead. It was mid-morning by Habitat time, but it'd been midnight ship time when she arrived. She'd come back and crash after finding a job.

Paying for a month's rent in advance had put a large dent in her cash card.

She briefly considered looking up the habitat's medical facility. Dr. Brodersen had recommending having a checkup when she got to her destination. But checking the scar in the bathroom mirror had shown it to be healing just fine. No redness, no swelling: just a four-inch reminder of Fulbright. For a few brief seconds, she let herself wonder what Jay was doing.

Settling in front of the comp, Jem accessed the habitat's public network and located the jobs section. She skipped over the medical, life-support, general administration, and waste management available positions. There were a fair number of retail, restaurant, and bar openings. *Yay.* Near the bottom of the list, she found *Miner's Paradise.* Her eyebrows rose, then drew down in a frown. That was some exceptionally high salaries posted, so why did they have so many openings? Looks like they'd have a waiting list for hiring.

Considering all the possible—and most likely—reasons for a bar's numerous openings that were avoided by locals, maybe *Miners Brawling* would be a better name. Jem hesitated, then clicked on the *Paradise's* link. Fifteen minutes later, she was heading to C-18 for her appointment with the owner. At the wages listed, she could deal with drunk miners for a month.

It didn't take five minutes for Jem to dislike Owen Testa, her new boss. He'd rudely sized her up, only asking if she'd ever waitressed and if her preg-shot was current. Not only was that last one highly personal, it made her hesitate before accepting the uniform he retrieved from a cabinet. Looking back, Jem realized that should have been her first clue.

It's only a month. It's only a month, Jem kept repeating as she returned to her room. She could aways quit if things got too rough. Then either find another job or just say 'the hell with it' and send for some of her Earth funds, all the while crossing her fingers that didn't attract the wrong attention. Stripping to her underwear, Jem fell on the bed. At least she'd have time to get some sleep before going to work tonight.

***

Jem dressed in the employee locker room, not wanting to wear the skimpy outfit through the corridors. The low-cut top was tight and calling the skirt 'short' was being generous. She'd have to remember to squat rather than bend over to pick something up.

The bartender was an immediate add to her dislike list. Bert Something-unpronounceable had leered at her half-exposed breasts when she went to pick up her tray and first order. She gave him a disgusted look. Her evening went downhill from there.

She was heading back toward the bar after serving her second table when she got pulled onto a guy's lap. "Excuse me?"

"Haven't seen you here before." His hand went up that short skirt.

Jem's eyes widened in outrage. She grabbed the guy's empty beer glass off the table and smacked him on top of the head with it. Good thing for him it was plastic.

"What the hell?" the guy sputtered as his table mates roared with laughter.

Jem twisted free. Stalking away, she heard one of them say, "Looks like Owen's got him a feisty one." Reaching the counter, she found Bert glaring at her.

"What did you do that for? They're *customers*."

"I'll serve them all the drinks they want, but no man is going to fondle me." Her jaw set at a brief flash of Dougson's hands groping her.

Bert started laughing. Hard. That should have been another clue.

By the fourth manhandling, Jem had figured a way to keep out of their laps and their hands to themselves. The final clues to what she'd gotten herself into was seeing how the other servers didn't stop the wandering hands. Stroked crotches, breasts, every- and anywhere. Jem stared, appalled, as one of the servers disappeared into a room down the hallway with a *customer*.

Note to self: find a new job tomorrow.

After two and a half hours of dodging and smacking hands, Jem headed for the restrooms. She needed a break. Her arm was grabbed before she could get in the door. Jerked roughly around, Jem found herself looking at a medium-sized man with narrow shoulders and cold eyes. Two scars crisscrossed his left cheek.

"Heard tell Owen had a new one. Good looking, good boobs, feisty but shy."

"Hands off of me," Jem snapped. *Isn't that a Security uniform?*

His gaze traveled over her, lingered on her breasts. He licked his lips. "We'll go to one of the private rooms."

"No."

"Wrong." He pulled her to him.

Jem's knee found the large bulge between his legs. She escaped into the bathroom as he collapsed. Staring into the mirror above a sink, she wondered if they'd follow her in. Nothing seemed off limits here.

The boss was waiting for her when she emerged. He grabbed her arm and pulled her into his office. Yelled at her for five minutes. Jem laid odds it was the guy she'd kneed who complained.

"You will go out there and provide the customers with whatever service they want. *Any* service. What did you expect when you hired on?"

"A bar, not a brothel," Jem retorted. "I'll serve drinks and they can finger their food. I am off-limits."

"How quaint," Testa sneered contemptuously, "and unrealistic. Three customers have requested you and a room." Jem's mouth dropped open. "Mr. Threader has requested—"

"I quit," Jem interrupted harshly. "Now. Immediately. You'll have your outfit as soon as I can get it off."

His features turned crafty. "Room two is open."

Like she'd walk in there. Turning, she headed for the locker room. Thank the universe she'd changed there. It only took a few minutes to peel herself out of the sex clothes. She hurriedly dressed in tunic and jeans, afraid of being cornered by one of the *customers* before she could get out. When she exited, her glowering ex-boss was waiting with arms crossed.

"Walk out of here and I'll have you blacklisted," he told her.

She tossed the clothes in his face and kept walking.

"You will regret this!" he yelled behind her.

I already do, Jem fumed, pushing her way out past several burly men coming in. And she thought this place would be better than Fulbright? Hah! First thing tomorrow, she was getting a ticket on the next ship out. Nor was she staying here a day longer than she had to. She'd even offer to work as ship crew if they didn't have an available passenger berth. Crap. Could she get a refund on her room?

Chapter 25

Jem stood in front of the Transport desk, giving the young girl behind it an appalled stare. "The next ship isn't scheduled for five *weeks*?"

"Yes ma'am. The habitat isn't on any major routes," she replied, apologetically. "Ellison maintains their half, though that mostly revolves around ore carriers and company personnel. We're primarily serviced by cargo ships that double as transports for the few that book passage here. Or leave. They're irregular at best. Last one came yesterday."

"Yeah, I was on it." *And should have stayed on it,* Jem thought sourly, as the girl's eyes widened. "Could I book passage on an Ellison ship?"

"No ma'am. They don't take non-company passengers or cargo."

"Fine. Do you offer a waiting list? Great. Add me to it."

"Name?"

"Jem Seaborne Wilmont."

Her fingers flew across the keyboard. "Arrivals are posted—" Voice and fingers froze. Her eyes rose, searched Jem's face for several seconds. "I can't."

"Why the hell not?"

"There's a hold against your name."

"Blacklisted?"

"Uh, no. This is a Security hold. The report says you're wanted for missing funds from *Miner's Paradise* and..." she cleared her throat, "....and assault."

Fury held Jem speechless for several seconds. "I only worked at that cesspit for a couple of hours," Jem said, her words clipped and harsh. "When I figured out exactly what his 'hiring for all positions' meant, I left. Without my pay or its funds. The *assault* was my knee applied to a don't-tell-me-no asshole."

A brief grin flickered across the girl's face. She glanced at her comp terminal. "A security alert has gone out." Her gaze met Jem's again and her head tilted slightly to the left.

Looking over, Jem saw a recessed door. Understanding what the girl meant, she gave her a "Thank you" and took off at a near run. She was about to open the door at the other end of a short hallway when she heard a harsh voice loudly demanding, *"Where's Jem Wilmont?"*

Jem yanked the door partially open as misdirection and *shifted*. The interior door slammed open and two large men in security uniforms barreled down the hallway and out into the main corridor. She watched as they strong-armed people or grabbed them and demanded 'where did she go?' All they could do was shake their heads. One guy got shoved face-first into a wall over his unappreciated response.

Jem hurried toward her room, guessing she'd need to find somewhere else to stay and preferably before she ran out of invisibility. *Yep, nailed it.* A guard lounged against her door, his gaze sweeping the corridor. *Want to bet my keycard won't open it?* No bet, her hindbrain snarked. No problem either, as Jem simply *phased* through the wall. Materializing, she threw the few things she'd unpacked back into her bags. Jem tossed the keycard on the small dresser, irritated at losing a month's worth of credits. Those security flags made showing up for a refund out of the question. *Shifting*, she went hunting for a quiet, reasonably clean hiding place.

Fortunately, the Mandoria Habitat had a number of empty rooms. Unfortunately, she nearly got caught in one that night. Evidently their very efficient monitoring system flagged the power utilization and a couple of security guys came to nab the unauthorized squatter. Luckily, arguing about some sport game as they unlocked the door alerted Jem in the bedroom and gave her time to collect her bags and *phase* away. She tried tucking herself into a corner of the Nature Preserve that stretched across the top C and D levels, only to learn that there were sensors covering every square meter. After that, she stuck to supply and storage areas, anywhere that had enough unmonitored space for her to hide in.

Apparently, management was more worried about people not paying rent or picking greenery off bushes and dwarf trees than pilfering, Jem observed sourly. When she did venture out, it was mostly for late-night trips to vending machines and bathrooms in unoccupied employee lounges. Especially after overhearing several of them taking bets on who would be the first. And not just for finding her.

What kind of management uses thugs and rapists as security? The kind that's probably no better than what she's seeing, that's what. And she was seeing a lot…overhearing even worse. No wonder the retail and office workers tended to travel in groups and avoided the more notorious areas. Like everything below Fourth Level, Section C.

What a mistake she'd made.

Brawls, including two that turned into bloody knife fights. Gaming and gambling dens. Places where the patrons didn't always bother taking the nude servers into a private area. Orgies. So-called *security* people making wagers on the fights instead of stopping them. Or accosting those they could catch alone or in out-of-the-way places. She'd come on one so-called 'guard' pushing a young girl into an alcove on E-7. There was no one else around to help the struggling girl, who looked barely sixteen. Jem had materialized and rushed to help. A double handful-of-hair yank pulled him back far enough for the girl to slide out and run. Jem slammed him into the wall and ran around the corner, *shifting* before the profusely cursing man barreled into view.

Why do people stay in this cesspit? The non-miners? Is the pay so good it outweighs the risk to them and family? Is it by choice, or were they somehow trapped here? Considering the lack of regular transport and her own experience, Jem decided to be generous and go with the latter reason. In the future, she would be sticking to planets or similarly large bodies that provided more options for both hiding and escape.

The waiting gave Jem time to think. To plan. Like sneaking back to Earth to visit Raj for that alias she'd foolishly turned down. He'd obviously had a better idea about her future needs than she'd had. Based on her current situation, that future would benefit from the occasional alternate identity. While there, she'd use her fat account to pay him and refill her cash card. Her regular one, not the big one she'd kept for any large pulls required for a skewer-Kurzvall plan.

In the meantime, she'd put a few credits back into her card to help get her back to Earth. She'd stood, *phased*, behind her ex-boss as he made several financial entries. Then found a bank kiosk and made a withdrawal from his account. Not a lot, just what the SOB owed her for the hours worked plus a little bit more as compensation for her current ordeal, since he'd set it in motion.

Yes, technically it was stealing, and Jem had winced at the memory of her outraged *"I am not a thief!"* response to Grathen's taunt. The circumstances here were exceptions, she'd promised herself.

***

Thank you, Universe! It had decided to be kind, only making her wait four days for deliverance. The *Rim Rangler* was snuggled up next to the habitat's docking arm. And, halleluiah, its first stop from here was Coleman Two, a decent planet with decent jobs. She'd been watching the ship unload cargo for the past two hours on a monitor. Jem wished the two rough-looking men and hard-eyed woman that had exited the access tube better luck than she'd had. Hoped they also knew what they were getting into.

Jem chewed her lip. *Phasing* was the only way she was getting on it.

She'd have roughly thirty minutes to get from her current hiding spot to the access tube, board the ship, and find a safe hidey-hole. According to the information posted, outgoing passengers wouldn't be boarded until just before it was ready to leave. She'd have to wait along with them. With all the activity going on, from prepping passenger rooms to cargo shuffling, it was too risky to *shift* and board sooner. A crewman might stumble across her during her post-shift vulnerability, when she was unable to go invisible.

It was going to be close.

She was on the same level as the docking arm but over half-way across the habitat, having been unable to find a closer monitoring spot this morning. Supply and cargo bays were busy all the time and activity triggered by the inbound ship had tripled it. *Okay, almost time.* Cargo containers were now moving from the habitat to the ship. Roughly twenty minutes later, Jem spotted the ship's cargo doors closing. *Yes.*

She cut the monitor off, tossed her backpack over her shoulder, took a firm grip on her travel bag, *shifted*, and ran. Maintenance carts, supply carts, whatever the hell that was, people—she did dodge a bit there—Jem grimly *phased* her way through. She plowed to a stop behind the passengers beginning to board. She really didn't want to go through seven people.

Not even winded, she thought with a chuckle.

Three men guarded the access tube, watching for her, no doubt. Two of them had taken up positions on either side of the tube and were scrutinizing each person as they moved forward. Even the men. *Really?* That would've been some disguise. She stuck her tongue out at the oblivious guard on her right as she passed him. The habitat's hatch swung shut behind her.

In the ship's plazo, Jem invisibly rode the lift up with a couple of them and then raced toward the ship's supply room. Seven passengers meant all the bunk rooms would be occupied. Good thing she was on a first-name basis with supply pallets. She felt the tell-tale tug as she *phased* into the room. Relief hit on finding no one in it. She'd gambled the crew would be busy with their departing tasks at this point.

Color bloomed and Jem felt her pulse racing. Excitement? Apprehension? Heart fixing to explode?

Surveying the room, Jem found a maze of stacked containers and cargo-netted boxes. *Excellent.* She tucked herself in behind a large stack of boxes labeled 'bathroom tissue.' Once she'd rested and could *shift* again, she'd snoop around and get a feel for the crew and passengers' movements, which, hopefully, would prevent an embarrassing bathroom moment. And if she did get caught—preferably with her guard down and not her pants? Jem mentally shrugged. She'd explain her situation. Not much they could do at that point. From what she'd heard, most crews didn't like stowaways and would hand them over to Law Enforcement as soon as they arrived at the next port. Given from where she'd escaped, maybe they'd settle for a stern warning.

Or a hearty congratulations.

Jem mulled outing herself, once safely in O-space, for about thirty seconds, then discarded it. She'd only risk the Enforcers if she had to. She pulled a chocolate bar and a bottle of water from her bag. She'd raided a vending machine down in E-19 last night and stuffed both bags. Less movement, less risk of being spotted. She'd also made quick use of a shower while down in maintenance. It'd be five days before she got another one on Coleman.

Settling back against the hull, Jem munched on her dinner and contemplated the past few months. Contemplated just how naïve and unprepared she'd been for this new life of hers. How many mistakes she'd made since leaving Earth. Both the Fulbright Station and the Mandoria Habitat had taught her valuable, if costly, lessons. What else awaited her?

A double chime sounded. It announced the O-drive activation and—*oh joy*—the throbbing at the base of her skull.

Chapter 26

The *Rim Rangler* was a Class IV Drone, its Cargo sub-designation and basic shape inherited from the workhorse of its ancestors, and was the largest of its class that was rated for both space and atmospheric operation. Lounge and kitchen sections behind the flight deck were the communal areas shared by both passengers and crew. Pocket-style doors opened on both sides of the hallway that ran from the kitchen to a supply/storage room at the other end. Behind them lay the bunkrooms and communal bathroom.

Directly beneath the flight deck was the plazo, a large open space that was the ship's main access/exit point. The area directly beneath the living areas held the ship's life blood, such as oxygen recycling and water and waste storage. A large cargo hold filled the remaining space between those living areas, both levels, and the engines.

Bored, restless, Jem decided to take a walk on the third ship day. *Phased*, of course.

She paused to stare wistfully at the food carousel, which was tucked between a standard freezer-cooler and four stacked microwaves. *Only two more days*, she consoled herself. Four people, two each crewmen and passengers, were playing cards at one of the long tables opposite the compact kitchen. Two more of her fellow passengers—the lucky stiffs— were having a late-evening meal on the other one. Continuing on through to the lounge, she found a couple watching what appeared to be an Earth

Medieval docu-history of some kind.

Jem stood in the doorway between the two areas for several minutes. A deep ache slowly grew within her as she listened to the conversations. To the laughter. The urge to just say 'the hell with it' and join them almost overwhelmed her. Almost. She reined it in brutally. *This is not helping.* She pivoted on her heel to go back to her hole.

She passed a crewman climbing out of a corner stairwell.

"Hey, John," one of the card-playing crewmen called out to him. "How's the captain doing?"

Jem paused at the hallway entrance, curious.

"Mostly okay," John replied. Walking over to the carousel, he started it rotating. Watching the food offerings pass, he added, "She still gets a bit splotchy-faced about it."

About what?

The crewman chuckled, threw down a card. "Yeah, she turned livid when I showed her the engine readouts when we were maneuvering away from the habitat."

One of the passenger card players cleared his throat. "There's something wrong with the engines?"

Jem's eyes widened. *Not what one wants to hear.*

"Nothing to worry about," the crewman replied quickly. "It's one of the ion engines."

John popped his selection into a microwave. Leaned back against the counter. "Our other five ions are more than enough to safely handle the ship. Captain Stowe is pissed because the *Rangler* came out of maintenance dock right before this run. They had to replace three of our Hermes engines, and they aren't cheap."

Hermes? Jem's attention sharpened. *Kurzvall's Hermes?*

The two diners exchanged a look. "What's happened?" the woman asked, sounding a bit nervous.

John tugged on his ear, then admitted, "The Number Two Ion became erratic on our approach to the Habitat. It flat out malfunctioned as we pulled away. From what the computer analysis shows, which we just went over for the umpteenth time, it must have picked up foreign bodies—dust, dirt, or pollen—at our last stop, which was Aribia Two."

A crewman grimaced. "Considering it's a mining dust ball, that wouldn't be hard."

The woman's companion frowned. "Aren't ion engines sealed?" he said.

Jem ignored the first warning tug.

"Yep," John said. "Hence the captain's pissed-off state since it's one of the new engines. It's obviously flawed. Probably no more than a hairline crack, but that's all it would take." The micro behind him dinged. Collecting silverware from a drawer, he settled down at the table.

"She should insist the company replace it with a new engine," one man said. "Free."

"Captain plans to," John said, ripping off his meal's cellophane covering. "But not until this run is completed. Two of our deliveries have no-later-than dates and we need to maintain our schedule."

"Not to mention reputation."

John pointed his fork at his fellow crewman. "That, too. In the meantime, we'll keep the Number Two shut down."

Jem lost the rest of the conversation as a second, stronger warning tugged. She mentally 'grabbed' that nebulous cord and held on as she rushed down the hallway. Felt it slipping. *No!* Felt it catch. She barely made it into the supply room when her invisibility fell away and she swayed. *Wow, that was*—Jem froze. The lights were on. Then a scraping sound came from her right. Carefully, as stealthy as she could, she sidled to the left and around a stacked pallet.

"Finally," someone grunted, followed by the slam of a container lid.

Peering through a crack, she watched a crewman come into view holding a medium-sized box. She held her breath as he walked to the door, perched it on his shoulder with one hand then flicked the lights off with the other one. The door *snicked* shut. Jem rested her forehead against the stack's netting. She waited for her pulse to settle and her legs to steady before worming her way back into her hole in a corner.

Feeling around in her bag, she pulled out a bottled water; it was her last one. Well, crap. With two days left to go, she was going to have to risk raiding the ship's cooler. She took a sip and slumped against the hull. Exhausted. More so than ever before. Was it because she'd actually fought to keep the *shift* from ending? Had she really given herself a few extra seconds?

Several deep breaths and half her water later, she pulled out her hand comp. The screen near blinded her when she turned it on. After her eyes adjusted, she pulled up Kurzvall's file and scrolled down his list of businesses. Yep, Hermes Ion Engines was one of his, and a major company at that. Hmmm. Eyes closed and head tilted back, her thoughts churned.

…small amounts of grit…*phased* delivery…

A smile slowly bloomed across Jem's face. She'd just figured out how to take down one of the murdering bastard's major revenue sources, one sabotaged engine at a time.

Chapter 27

Her first stop after landing at the LaGrange Spaceport was a transit dorm in the Port Circle where she took a long, hot shower. That was followed by a full, freshly prepared meal in a nearby restaurant. It was amazing how normal, mundane things could become luxuries. Buoyed, Jem headed for the Coleman Intersystem Bank.

LaGrange, Coleman Two, was a busy, fast-growing planet. The bank teller didn't bat an eye when Jem arranged to have a hundred thousand credits—ten thousand dollars—transferred from her Earth bank account. Impatient to get back to Earth and Raj, she'd opted to risk that rather than spend the weeks necessary to earn the money for passage. Regular passage, instead of the gut-clenching tension of hiding.

That was four days ago. Now, she was there to pick up her money, having been notified of its deposit into her temp account. Jem politely declined their offer to convert it into a permanent account, instead closing it after downloading the credits into her cash card. She walked out, feeling better than she had in weeks. *Yay, Earth. Here I come.* Her euphoria lasted until halfway down the LaGrange Spaceport's crowded main terminal.

Dougson. Talking with two beefy men in front of the Pan-Star Line counter.

Jem whipped around. Heart pounding, she managed to walk sedately back the way she'd came. Reaching the terminal entrance, Jem snuck a look over her shoulder. No sign of pursuit. She gave her braid a hard tug.

Crossing paths with Kurzvall's head thug had to happen sooner or later but, dammit, was it her fund transfer request? Was that how he'd tracked her? Big coincidence in a big galaxy if not. Exactly what she'd been afraid of, and why she'd resisted doing it before.

At least she had seen them first.

She stepped out into the late afternoon light. What now? As soon as they started searching, asking about her…it wouldn't take long. She hadn't been wearing her contacts. Did she dare purchase a ticket now? Would he have the passenger lists watched? Dammit. She needed that alias. She needed to get to Earth. Fast. But…*oh*. That would do it.

Jem licked suddenly dry lips.

The UPMS's autonomous drones, averaging seven meters long from engine base to electronic nose, took advantage of the Otanak Drive's size-versus-time quirk. One of them should get her to Earth in about eight hours or so, instead of the days or weeks a regular ship would need, depending on its size. Remembering the last time she'd been in a UPMS mail pod had her hands twitching. *Ugh!*

Decision made, Jem took a taxi to her hotel. She was packed and checked out in under twenty minutes. From there, she took a public bus back the spaceport, to the Universal Postal and Messaging Service main terminal where she paid cash for a courier configuration. Ten minutes later, she was ordering coffee and pie in a small adjacent café, as she'd been told it'd take about forty-five minutes to convert the mail pod for her. Jem had nearly offered to do it for them in thirty, but discretion won out.

Even though she didn't expect them, Jem kept an unobtrusive eye on the café's door for her stalkers while enjoying a very delicious slice of unpronounceable goodness. *Xnthryndaey berries?* In fact, since she had the time, she ordered a second one. Asking the server how to pronounce it, she got 'ze-NTH-roan-day.'

Must be a Coleman native fruit, but who the hell named it that?

As the minutes ticked away, Jem's muscles wound tighter. According to the bored clerk, UPMS Earth-transit time from Coleman was just under six hours. *Relax. You can handle the pod. Think about what comes after Earth instead.*

Oh, yeah!

The Orion System: her first thorn in Kurzvall's hide. She was going to expose his underhanded and illegal fixed-contract arrangement with that System Senator. It should be fairly easy to gather the information proving it. Then, after Orion, she'd go after his Hermes engine company. That thorn would be more difficult and take longer, but its collapse would be *spectacular*—a sly grin worked its way across her face—and *painful* for Kurzvall.

After that, who knows?

Jem finished her coffee. Gathering up her two bags, she exited the café and headed toward the UPMS terminal, her steps light. Determined. She'd deal with the future and its consequences when it got here. For now, she'd use her invisibility, her phasing, in whatever way needed to accomplish her goals. By the time she finished with Reginal Kurzvall the Bastard, he'd be bleeding—metaphorically—as if dragged through a cactus patch.

She was *soooo* looking forward to it.

Titles by R. D. Chapman

<u>Blurring Reality Series</u>

Shattered Reality
Blurring Reality
Tangled Reality
Reality Kicked

<u>D'Accio Investigations Series</u>

At Any Cost

About the Author

R. D. Chapman has been an avid reader all her life. A retired empty-nester living quietly in Nebraska with her husband, she draws on a lifetime of experience ranging from cook to software developer to craft characters and stories. She writes in a blend of SF&F, urban fantasy, and mystery with a smidgen of humor and romance. When not writing, she loves spending time with the three Rs: Reading, cRocheting, and Relaxing.

* * * * *

Thank you for reading *Shattered Reality*. If you enjoyed this, please consider leaving a review, as they are essential to expanding my sales and readership. Even a few simple lines will help. Thanks!